Disney RALPH BREAKS THE INTERNET

NO LONGER PROPERTY OF
ANYTHINK LIBRARIES/
RANGEVIEW LIBRARY DISTRICT

Click Start
A Select-Your-Story Adventure

SCRIPT BY Joe Caramagna LAYOUT BY Emilio Urbano
CLEAN UP AND INKS BY Andrea Greppi, Marco Forcelloni, Michela Frare
COLORING BY Angela Capolupo, Giuseppe Fontana, Massimo Rocca
LETTERING BY Chris Dickey

Heart from the Start, Eyes on the Prize

SCRIPT AND PENCILS BY Amy Mebberson
CLEAN UP AND INKS BY Michela Frare COLORING BY Dan Jackson
LETTERING BY Richard Starkings AND Comicraft's Jimmy Betancourt

COVER ART BY
Emilio Urbano, Andrea Greppi, Angela Capolupo

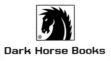

Dark Horse Books

DARK HORSE BOOKS

president and publisher **Mike Richardson**
collection editor **Freddye Miller**
collection assistant editor **Judy Khuu**
designer **David Nestelle, Chris Dickey**
digital art technician **Samantha Hummer**

Neil Hankerson Executive Vice President • Tom Weddle Chief Financial Officer • Randy Stradley Vice President of Publishing • Nick McWhorter Chief Business Development Officer • Dale LaFountain Chief Information Officer • Matt Parkinson Vice President of Marketing • Cara Niece Vice President of Production and Scheduling • Mark Bernardi Vice President of Book Trade and Digital Sales • Ken Lizzi General Counsel • Dave Marshall Editor in Chief • Davey Estrada Editorial Director • Chris Warner Senior Books Editor • Cary Grazzini Director of Specialty Projects • Lia Ribacchi Art Director • Vanessa Todd-Holmes Director of Print Purchasing • Matt Dryer Director of Digital Art and Prepress • Michael Gombos Director of International Publishing and Licensing • Kari Yadro Director of Custom Programs • Kari Torson Director of International Licensing

DISNEY PUBLISHING WORLDWIDE GLOBAL MAGAZINES, COMICS AND PARTWORKS
PUBLISHER Lynn Waggoner • EDITORIAL TEAM Bianca Coletti (Director, Magazines), Guido Frazzini (Director, Comics), Carlotta Quattrocolo (Executive Editor), Stefano Ambrosio (Executive Editor, New IP), Camilla Vedove (Senior Manager, Editorial Development), Behnoosh Khalili (Senior Editor), Julie Dorris (Senior Editor—Click Start Project Lead), Mina Riazi (Assistant Editor), Jonathan Manning (Assistant Editor) • DESIGN Enrico Soave (Senior Designer) • ART Ken Shue (VP, Global Art), Manny Mederos (Senior Illustration Manager, Comics and Magazines), Roberto Santillo (Creative Director), Marco Ghiglione (Creative Manager), Stefano Attardi (Computer Art Designer) • PORTFOLIO MANAGEMENT Olivia Ciancarelli (Director) • BUSINESS & MARKETING Mariantonietta Galla (Marketing Manager), Virpi Korhonen (Editorial Manager)

SPECIAL THANKS to Rich Moore, Phil Johnston, Clark Spencer, Jim Reardon, Cory Loftis, Matthias Lechner, Ami Thompson, Stevi Carter, Brittany Kikuchi, Simona Grandi, Jeff Clark, Alison Giordano, and Luca Pisanu.

Ralph Breaks the Internet: Click Start—A Select-Your-Story Adventure

Published by Dark Horse Books
A division of Dark Horse Comics, Inc.
10956 SE Main Street
Milwaukie, OR 97222

DarkHorse.com

To find a comics shop in your area, visit comicshoplocator.com

First edition: December 2018
ISBN 978-1-50671-150-8
Digital ISBN 978-1-50671-155-3

1 3 5 7 9 10 8 6 4 2
Printed in the United States of America

Meet the Players!

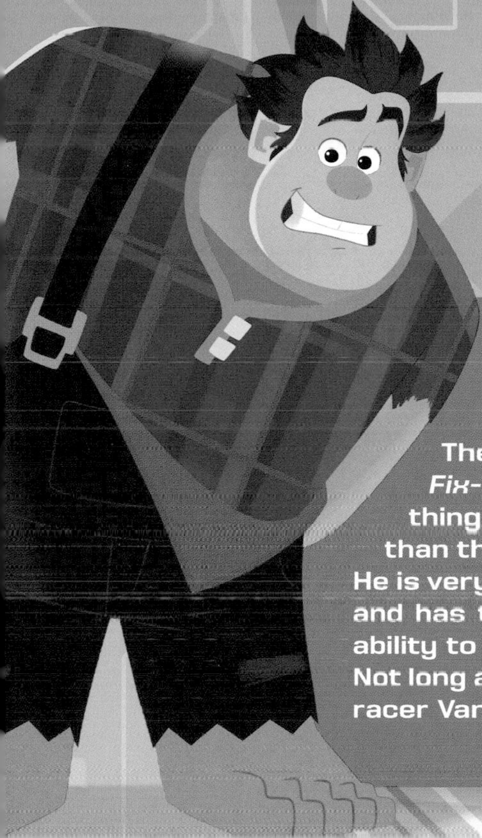

Wreck-It Ralph

The Bad Guy from the 8-bit video game, *Fix-It Felix, Jr.* Ralph's job is to wreck all things in Niceland. But Ralph is much more than the role he plays, and he's not a *bad* guy. He is very talented at wrecking things, however, and has to be careful to make sure to use his ability to his advantage—and to everyone else's. Not long ago, Ralph found his best friend forever, racer Vanellope von Schweetz.

Vanellope von Schweetz

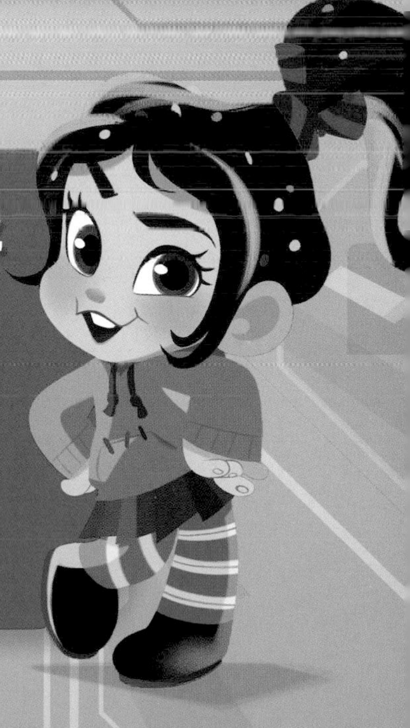

The best racer in the candy kart racing game, *Sugar Rush*. Vanellope is sharp-witted, spunky, and fun-loving, and she shows no pretension when it comes to being a princess. Vanellope has been setting the track on fire ever since Wreck-It Ralph visited her game and helped her to regain her rightful place as ruler of *Sugar Rush*. And while she loves her race, she longs for something different . . .

Now, let's go to the internet!

Welcome to the internet, friendo!

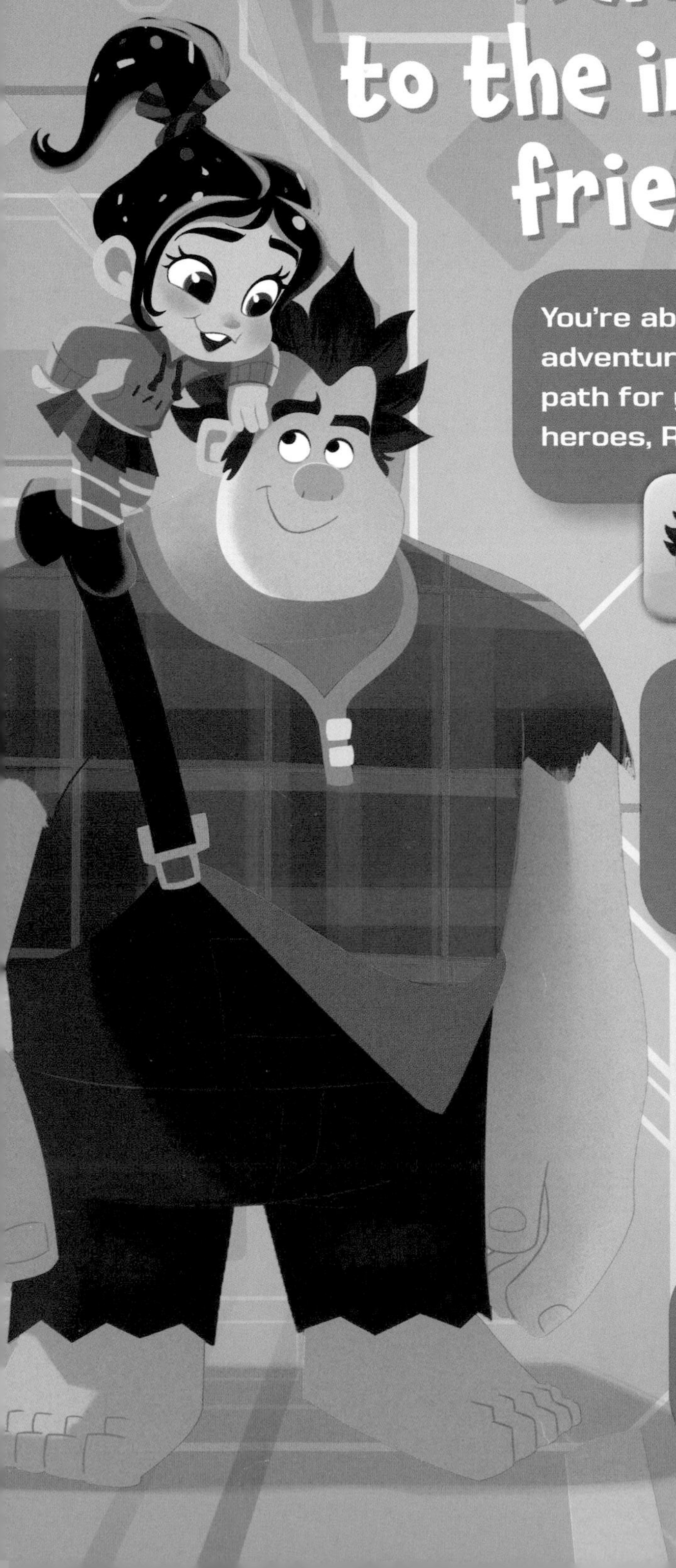

You're about to enter a fun-filled adventure where *you* choose a path for your favorite video game heroes, Ralph and Vanellope.

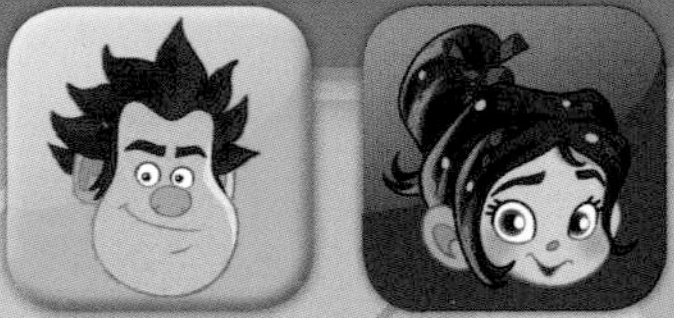

To select your own story, all you have to do is follow the instruction icons at the bottom of each page and make your choice!

To begin selecting your story, click START

START
GO TO PAGE 7

To skip to Vanellope's adventure in Oh My Disney, click SKIP

SKIP
GO TO PAGE 55

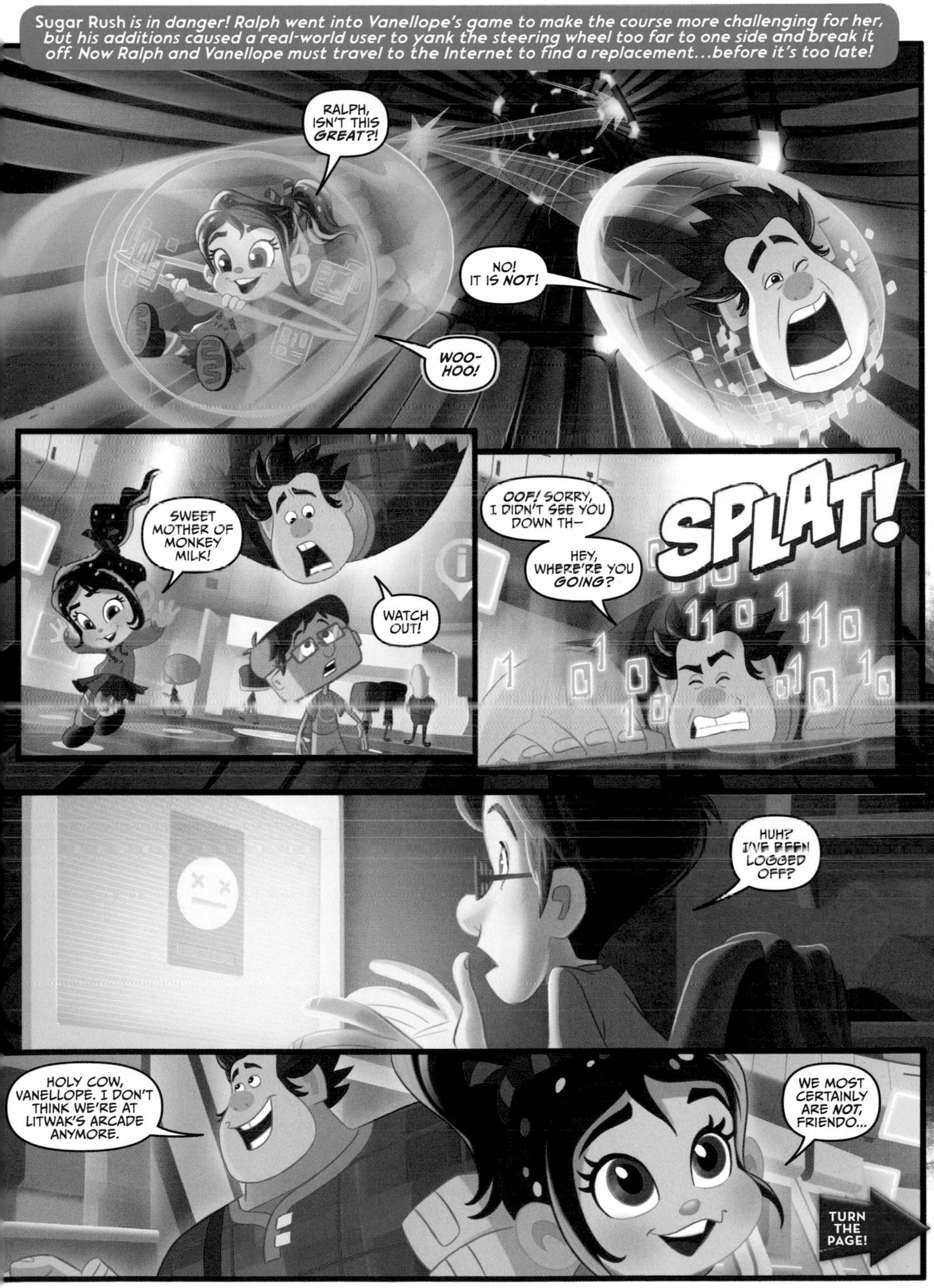
Sugar Rush is in danger! Ralph went into Vanellope's game to make the course more challenging for her, but his additions caused a real-world user to yank the steering wheel too far to one side and break it off. Now Ralph and Vanellope must travel to the Internet to find a replacement...before it's too late!
RALPH, ISN'T THIS GREAT?!
NO! IT IS NOT!
WOO-HOO!
SWEET MOTHER OF MONKEY MILK!
WATCH OUT!
OOF! SORRY, I DIDN'T SEE YOU DOWN TH—
SPLAT!
HEY, WHERE'RE YOU GOING?
HUH? I'VE BEEN LOGGED OFF?
HOLY COW, VANELLOPE. I DON'T THINK WE'RE AT LITWAK'S ARCADE ANYMORE.
WE MOST CERTAINLY ARE NOT, FRIENDO...
TURN THE PAGE!

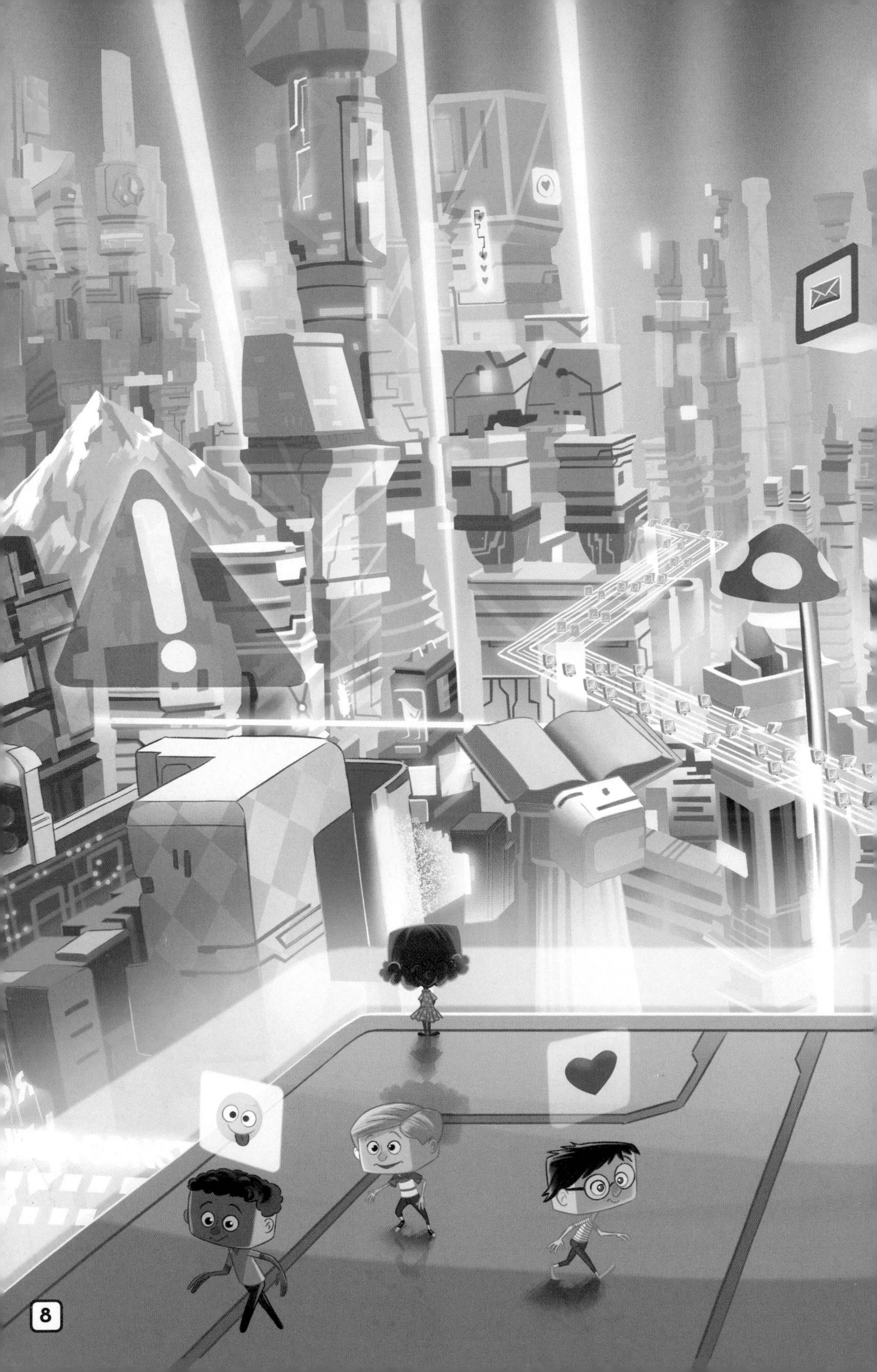

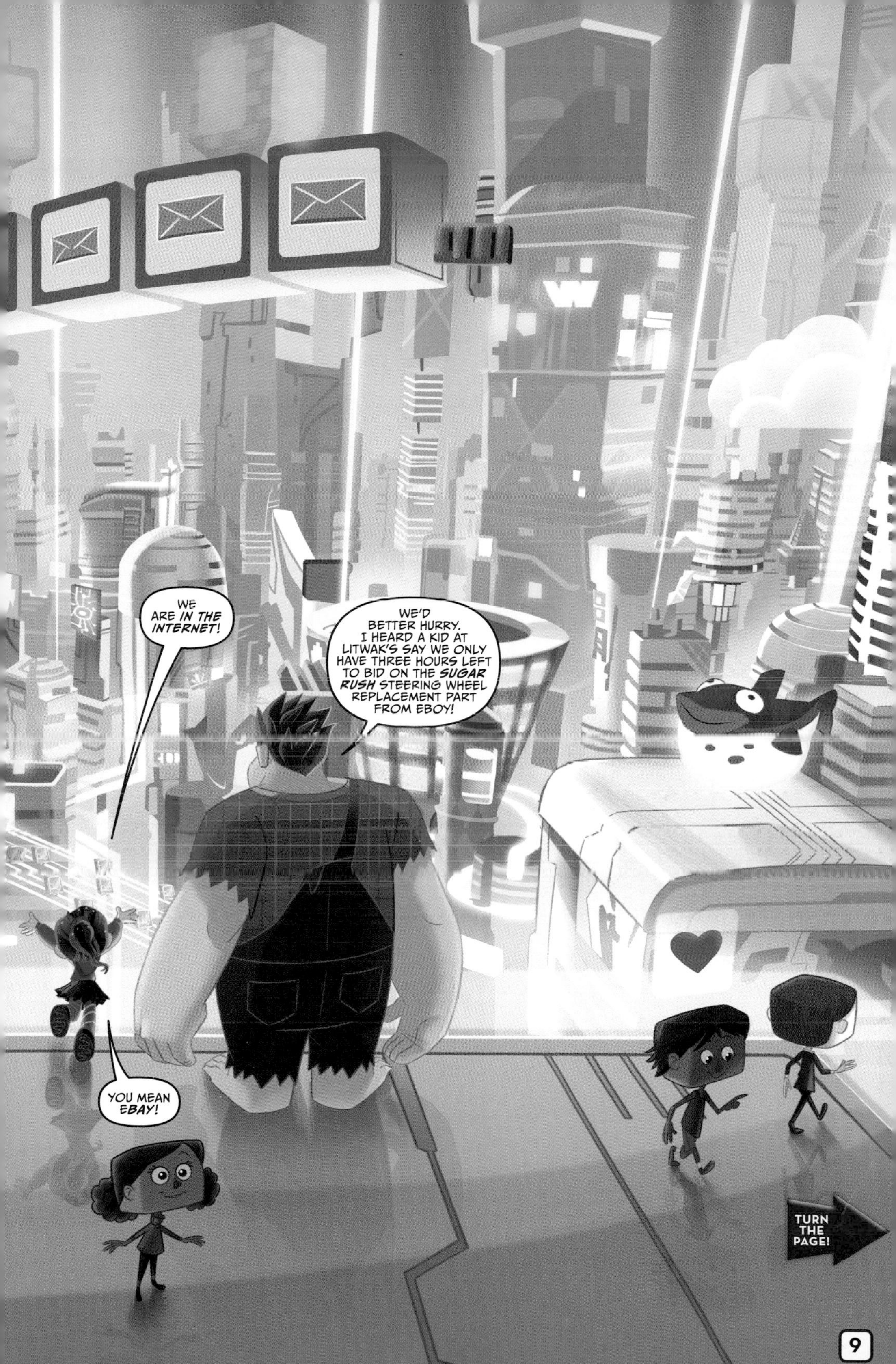
WE ARE IN THE INTERNET!
WE'D BETTER HURRY. I HEARD A KID AT LITWAK'S SAY WE ONLY HAVE THREE HOURS LEFT TO BID ON THE SUGAR RUSH STEERING WHEEL REPLACEMENT PART FROM EBOY!
YOU MEAN EBAY!
TURN THE PAGE!

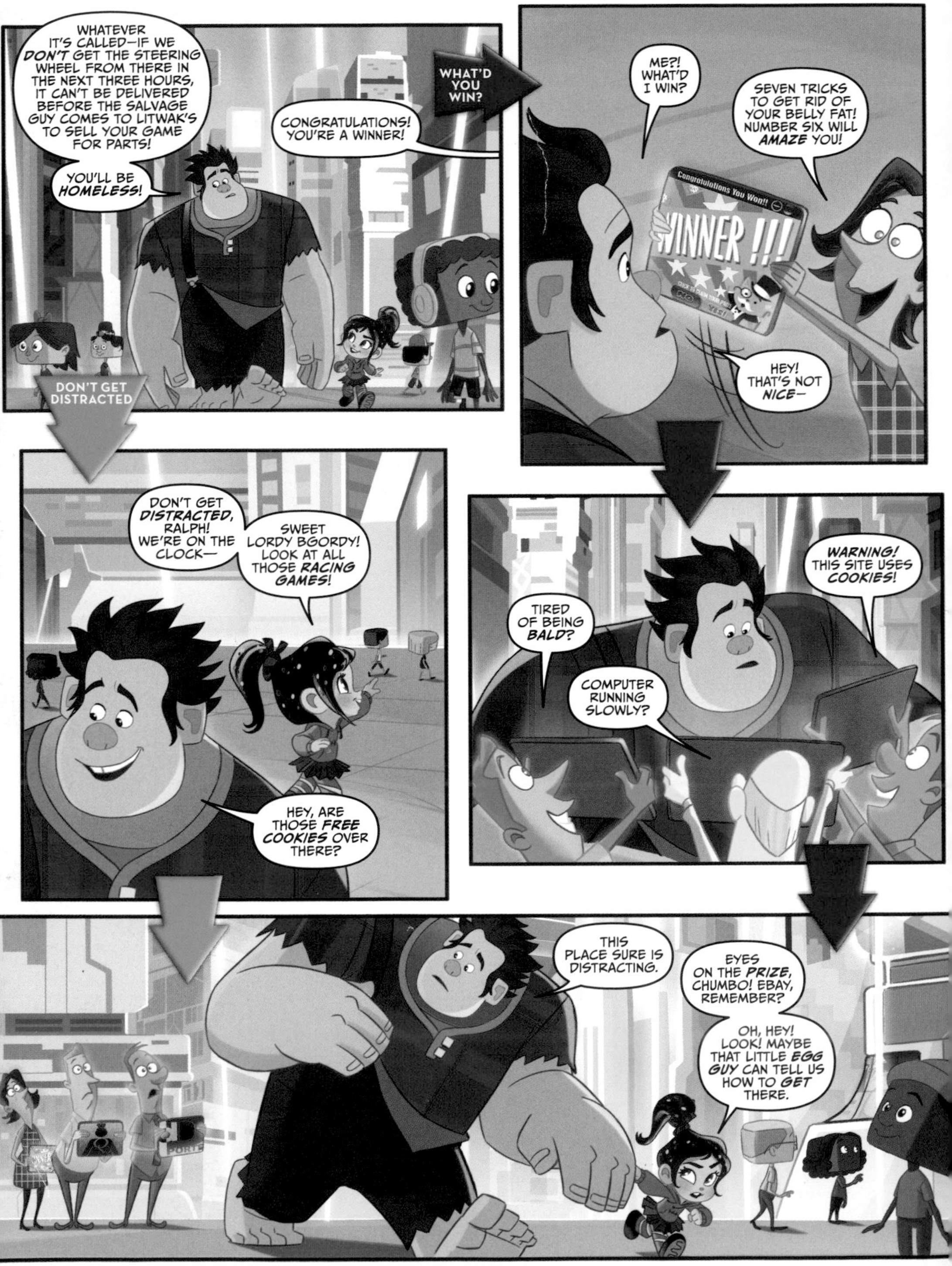

WHATEVER IT'S CALLED—IF WE DON'T GET THE STEERING WHEEL FROM THERE IN THE NEXT THREE HOURS, IT CAN'T BE DELIVERED BEFORE THE SALVAGE GUY COMES TO LITWAK'S TO SELL YOUR GAME FOR PARTS!
YOU'LL BE HOMELESS!
CONGRATULATIONS! YOU'RE A WINNER!
WHAT'D YOU WIN?
ME?! WHAT'D I WIN?
SEVEN TRICKS TO GET RID OF YOUR BELLY FAT! NUMBER SIX WILL AMAZE YOU!
Congratulations You Won!!
WINNER !!!
NO
YES!
HEY! THAT'S NOT NICE—
DON'T GET DISTRACTED
DON'T GET DISTRACTED, RALPH! WE'RE ON THE CLOCK—
SWEET LORDY BGORDY! LOOK AT ALL THOSE RACING GAMES!
HEY, ARE THOSE FREE COOKIES OVER THERE?
TIRED OF BEING BALD?
WARNING! THIS SITE USES COOKIES!
COMPUTER RUNNING SLOWLY?
THIS PLACE SURE IS DISTRACTING.
EYES ON THE PRIZE, CHUMBO! EBAY, REMEMBER?
OH, HEY! LOOK! MAYBE THAT LITTLE EGG GUY CAN TELL US HOW TO GET THERE.

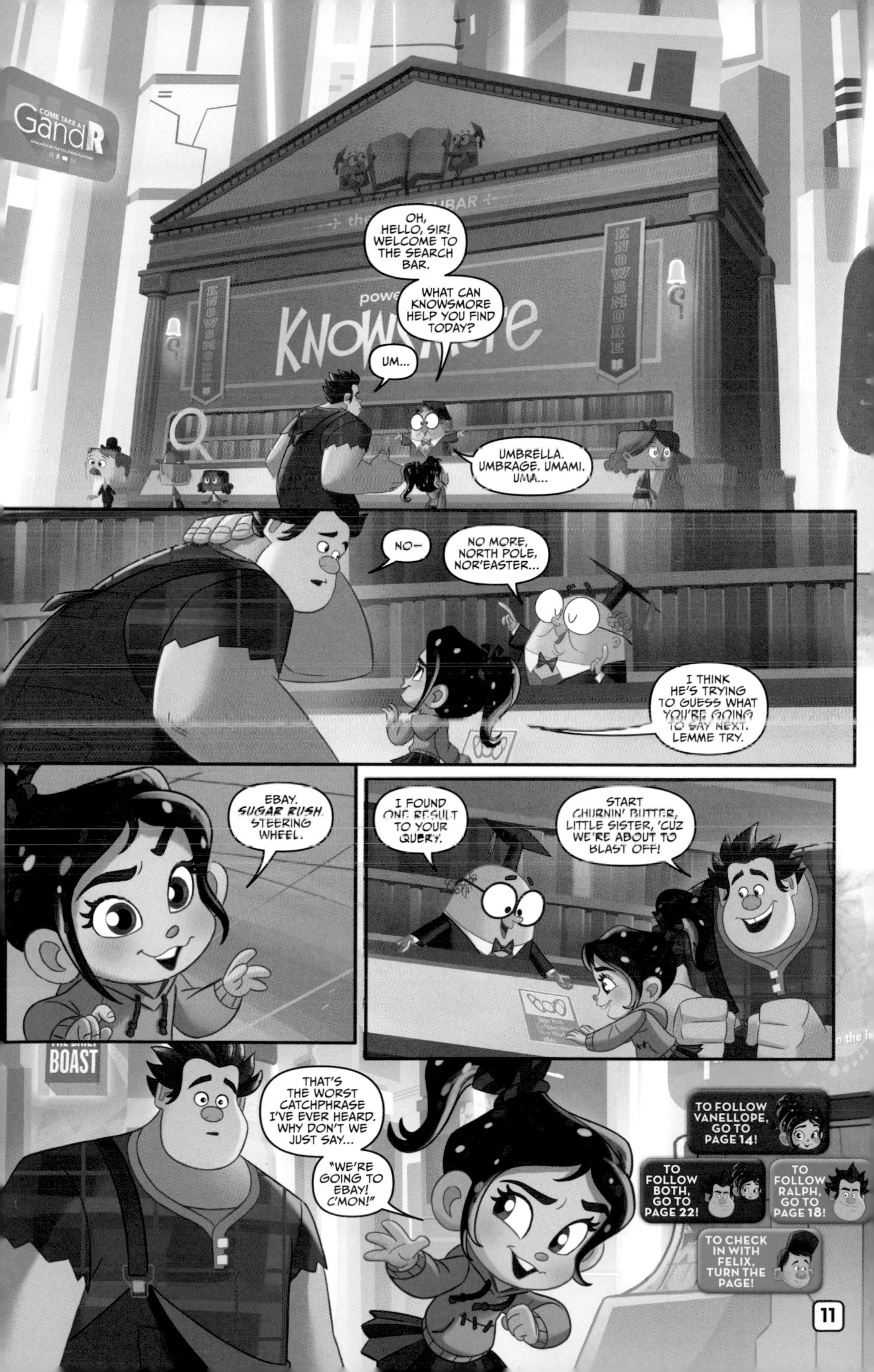
COME TAKE A GandR
BOASTUBAR
KNOWSMORE
OH, HELLO, SIR! WELCOME TO THE SEARCH BAR.
WHAT CAN KNOWSMORE HELP YOU FIND TODAY?
UM...
UMBRELLA. UMBRAGE. UMAMI. UMA...
NO–
NO MORE, NORTH POLE, NOR'EASTER...
I THINK HE'S TRYING TO GUESS WHAT YOU'RE GOING TO SAY NEXT. LEMME TRY.
EBAY. *SUGAR RUSH* STEERING WHEEL.
I FOUND ONE RESULT TO YOUR QUERY.
START CHURNIN' BUTTER, LITTLE SISTER, 'CUZ WE'RE ABOUT TO BLAST OFF!
BOAST
THAT'S THE WORST CATCHPHRASE I'VE EVER HEARD. WHY DON'T WE JUST SAY...
"WE'RE GOING TO EBAY! C'MON!"
TO FOLLOW VANELLOPE, GO TO PAGE 14!
TO FOLLOW BOTH, GO TO PAGE 22!
TO FOLLOW RALPH, GO TO PAGE 18!
TO CHECK IN WITH FELIX, TURN THE PAGE!

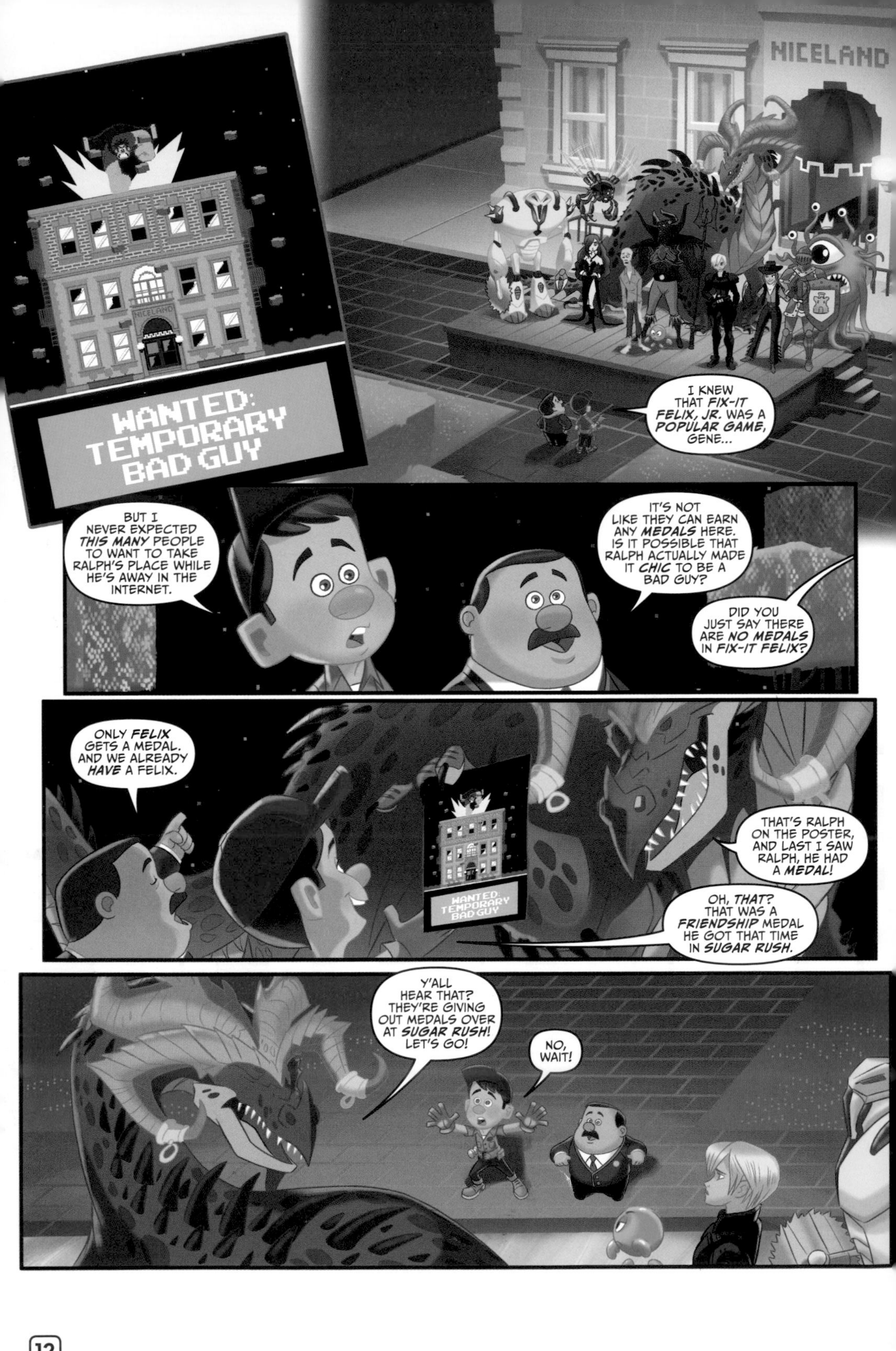
NICELAND
WANTED: TEMPORARY BAD GUY
I KNEW THAT FIX-IT FELIX, JR. WAS A POPULAR GAME, GENE...
BUT I NEVER EXPECTED THIS MANY PEOPLE TO WANT TO TAKE RALPH'S PLACE WHILE HE'S AWAY IN THE INTERNET.
IT'S NOT LIKE THEY CAN EARN ANY MEDALS HERE. IS IT POSSIBLE THAT RALPH ACTUALLY MADE IT CHIC TO BE A BAD GUY?
DID YOU JUST SAY THERE ARE NO MEDALS IN FIX-IT FELIX?
ONLY FELIX GETS A MEDAL. AND WE ALREADY HAVE A FELIX.
WANTED: TEMPORARY BAD GUY
THAT'S RALPH ON THE POSTER, AND LAST I SAW RALPH, HE HAD A MEDAL!
OH, THAT? THAT WAS A FRIENDSHIP MEDAL HE GOT THAT TIME IN SUGAR RUSH.
Y'ALL HEAR THAT? THEY'RE GIVING OUT MEDALS OVER AT SUGAR RUSH! LET'S GO!
NO, WAIT!

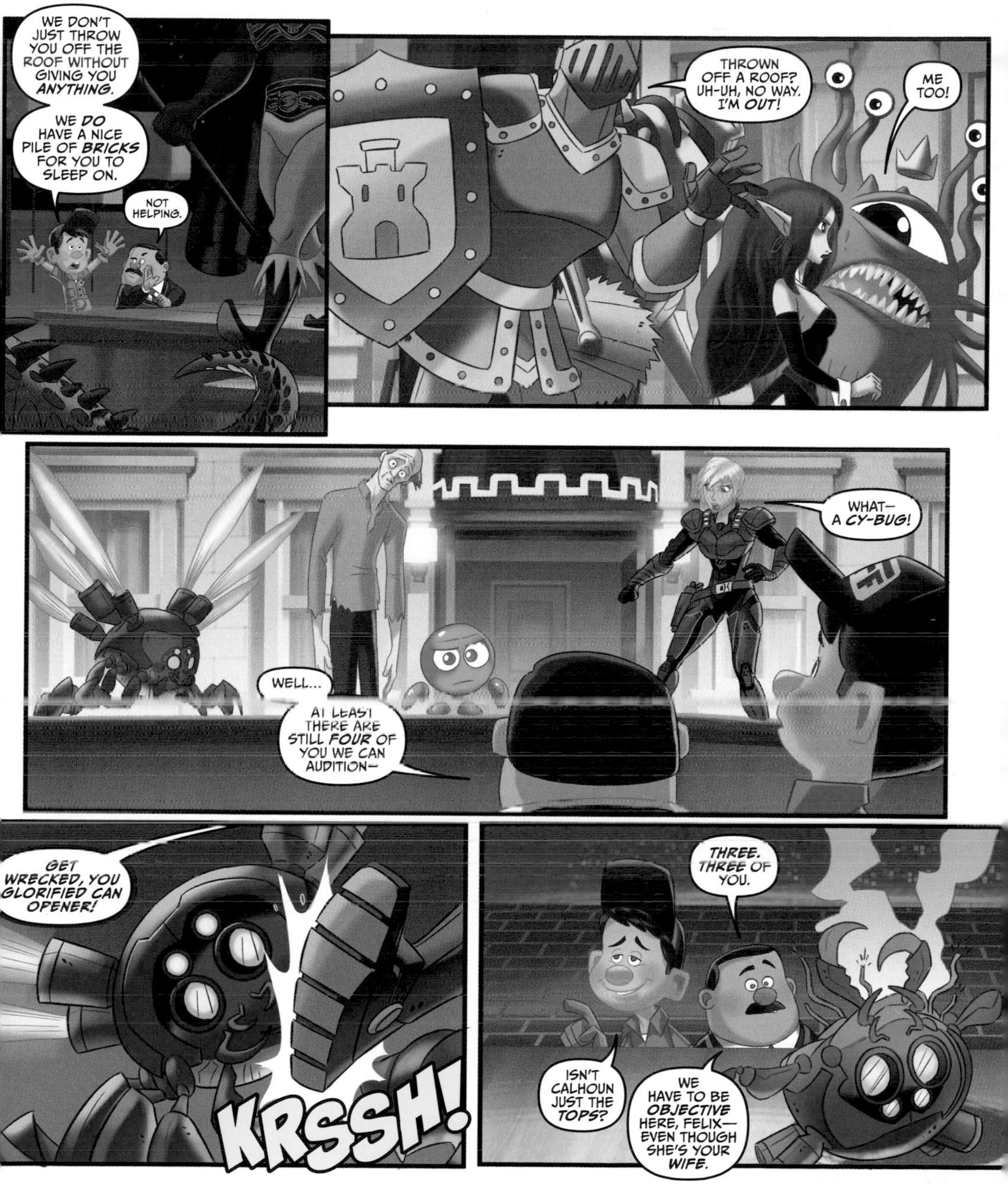

WE DON'T JUST THROW YOU OFF THE ROOF WITHOUT GIVING YOU *ANYTHING*.
WE *DO* HAVE A NICE PILE OF *BRICKS* FOR YOU TO SLEEP ON.
NOT HELPING.
THROWN OFF A ROOF? UH-UH, NO WAY. I'M *OUT*!
ME TOO!
WHAT— A *CY-BUG*!
WELL...
AT LEAST THERE ARE STILL *FOUR* OF YOU WE CAN AUDITION—
GET WRECKED, YOU GLORIFIED CAN OPENER!
KRSSH!
THREE. THREE OF YOU.
ISN'T CALHOUN JUST THE *TOPS*?
WE HAVE TO BE *OBJECTIVE* HERE, FELIX— EVEN THOUGH SHE'S YOUR *WIFE*.

TO AUDITION ZOMBIE, GO TO PAGE 24!

TO AUDITION SOUR BILL, GO TO PAGE 30!

TO AUDITION CALHOUN, GO TO PAGE 38!

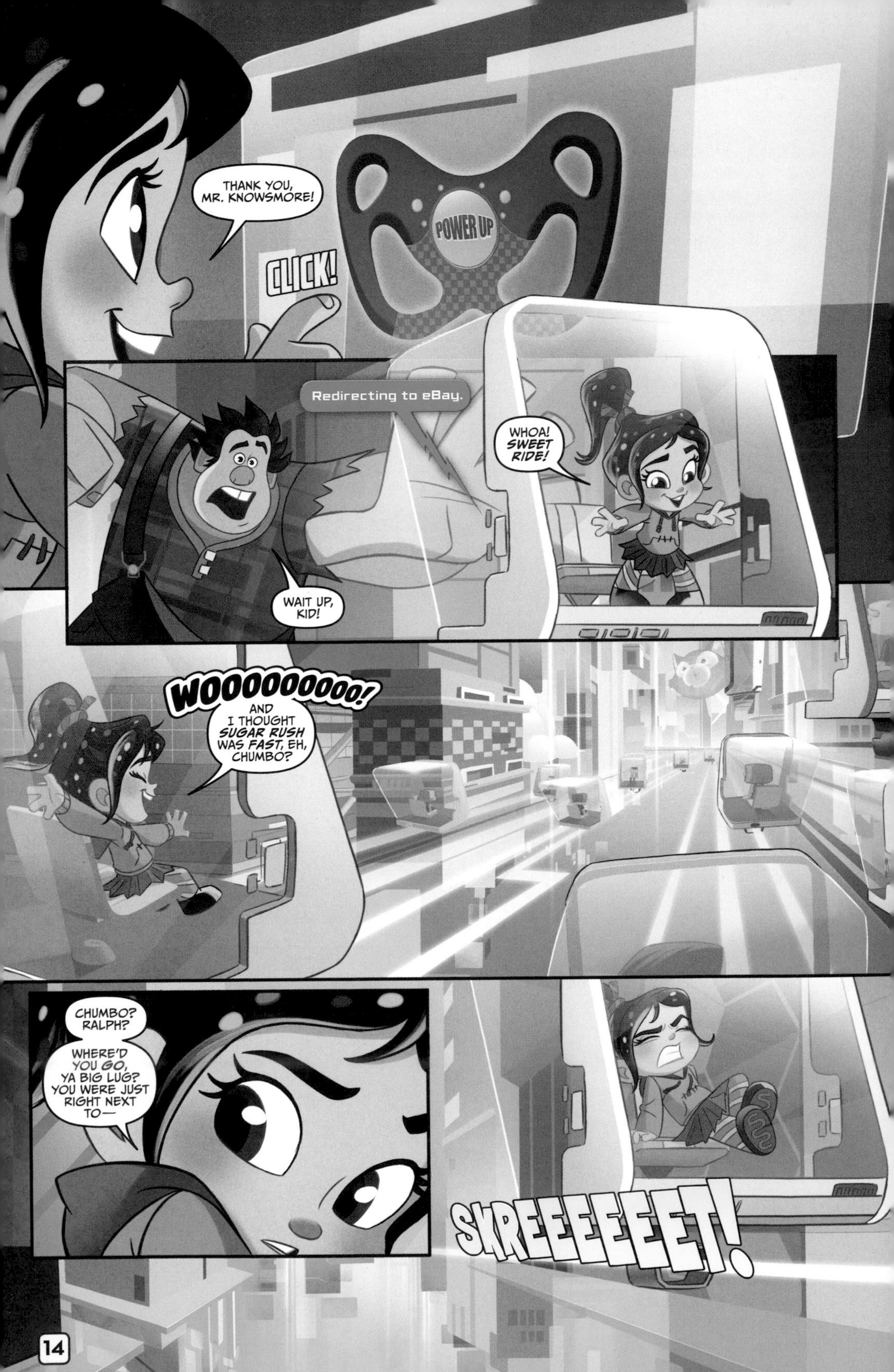
THANK YOU, MR. KNOWSMORE!
CLICK!
POWER UP
Redirecting to eBay.
WAIT UP, KID!
WHOA! SWEET RIDE!
WOOOOOOOOO!
AND I THOUGHT SUGAR RUSH WAS FAST, EH, CHUMBO?
CHUMBO? RALPH?
WHERE'D YOU GO, YA BIG LUG? YOU WERE JUST RIGHT NEXT TO—
SKREEEEEEET!

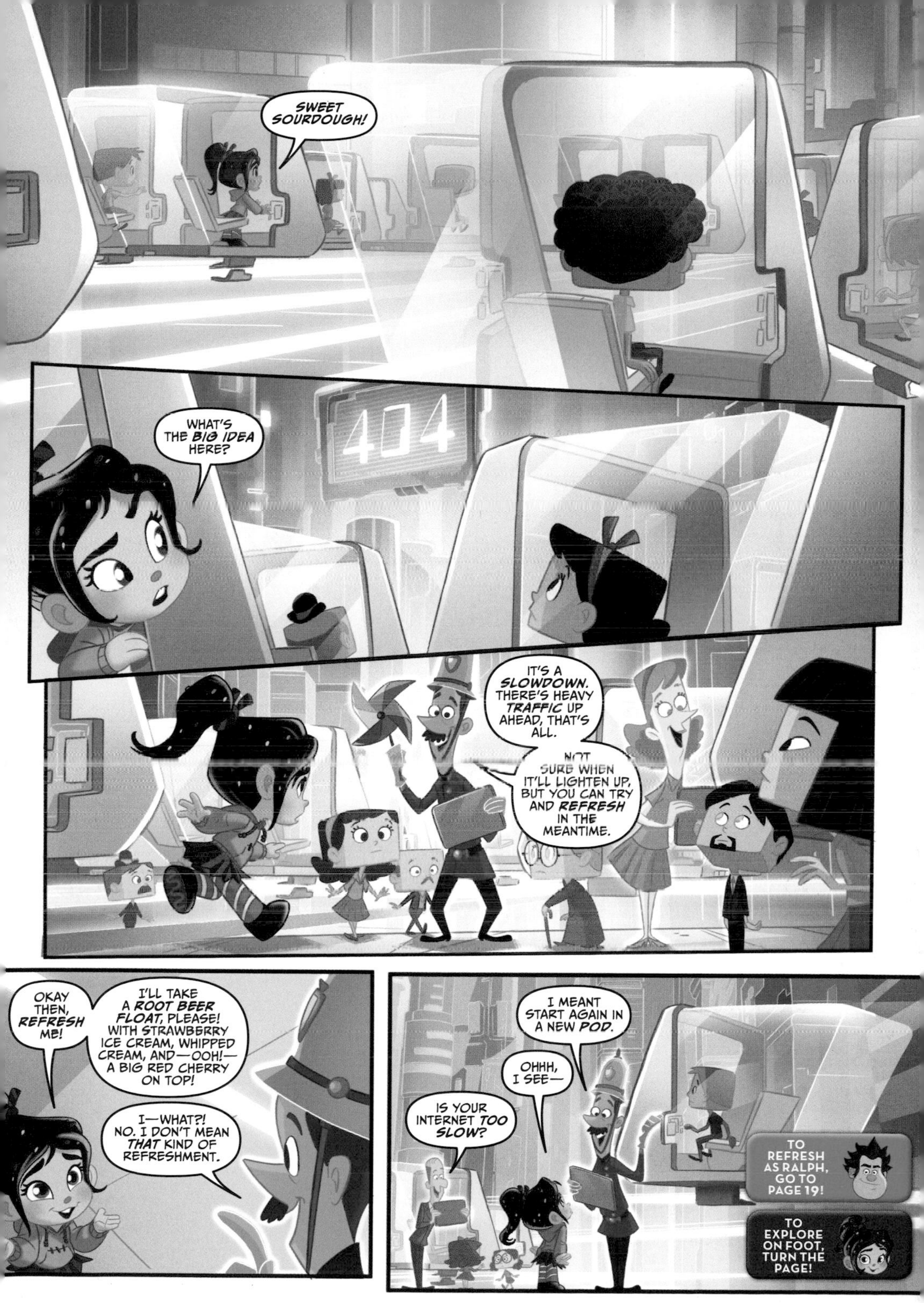

SWEET SOURDOUGH!
WHAT'S THE BIG IDEA HERE?
404
IT'S A SLOWDOWN. THERE'S HEAVY TRAFFIC UP AHEAD, THAT'S ALL.
NOT SURE WHEN IT'LL LIGHTEN UP, BUT YOU CAN TRY AND REFRESH IN THE MEANTIME.
OKAY THEN, REFRESH ME!
I'LL TAKE A ROOT BEER FLOAT, PLEASE! WITH STRAWBERRY ICE CREAM, WHIPPED CREAM, AND—OOH!—A BIG RED CHERRY ON TOP!
I—WHAT?! NO. I DON'T MEAN THAT KIND OF REFRESHMENT.
I MEANT START AGAIN IN A NEW POD.
OHHH, I SEE—
IS YOUR INTERNET TOO SLOW?

TO REFRESH AS RALPH, GO TO PAGE 19!
TO EXPLORE ON FOOT, TURN THE PAGE!

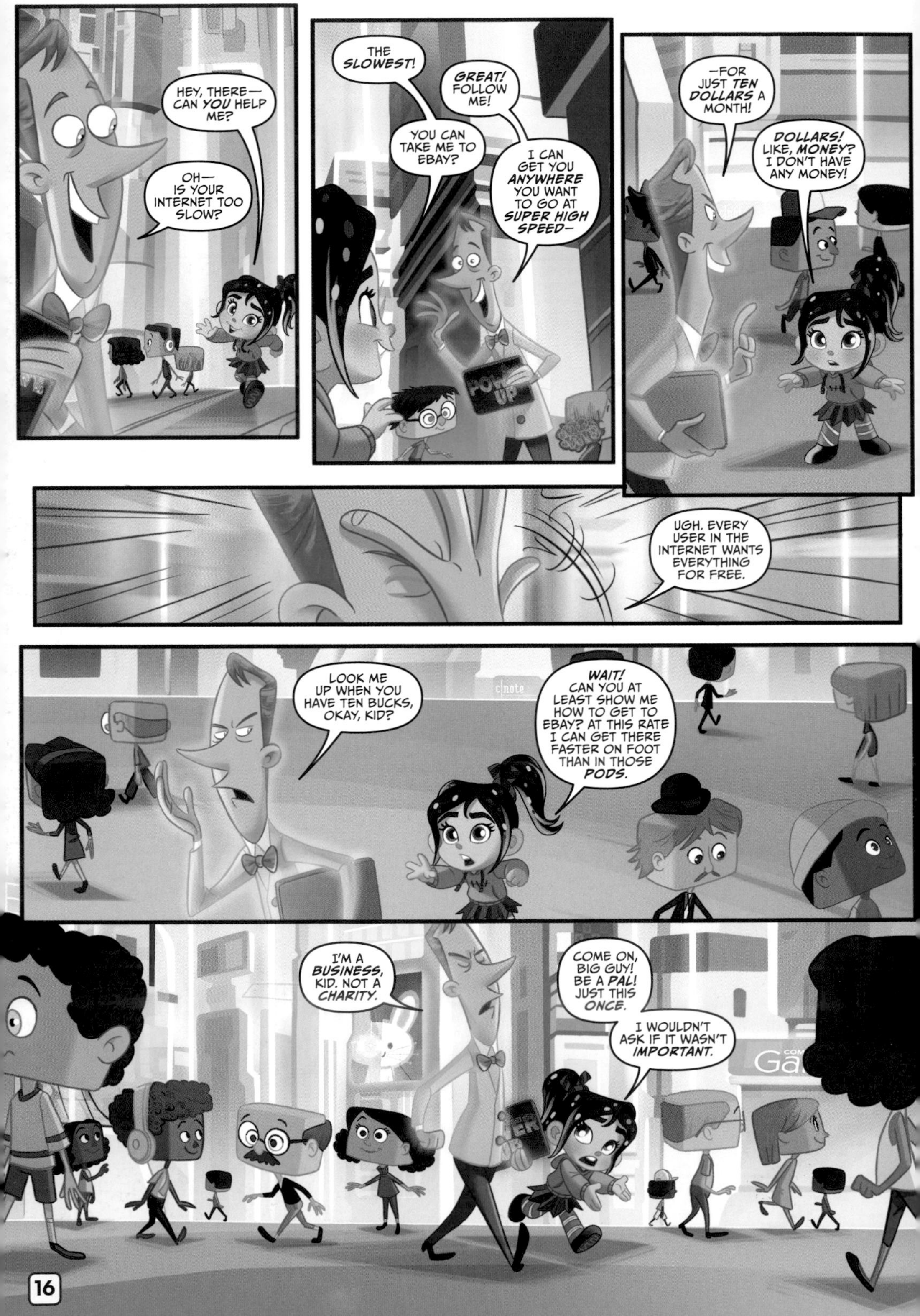
HEY, THERE— CAN YOU HELP ME?
OH— IS YOUR INTERNET TOO SLOW?
THE SLOWEST!
GREAT! FOLLOW ME!
YOU CAN TAKE ME TO EBAY?
I CAN GET YOU ANYWHERE YOU WANT TO GO AT SUPER HIGH SPEED—
POW UP
—FOR JUST TEN DOLLARS A MONTH!
DOLLARS! LIKE, MONEY? I DON'T HAVE ANY MONEY!
UGH. EVERY USER IN THE INTERNET WANTS EVERYTHING FOR FREE.
LOOK ME UP WHEN YOU HAVE TEN BUCKS, OKAY, KID?
c|note
WAIT! CAN YOU AT LEAST SHOW ME HOW TO GET TO EBAY? AT THIS RATE I CAN GET THERE FASTER ON FOOT THAN IN THOSE PODS.
I'M A BUSINESS, KID. NOT A CHARITY.
COME ON, BIG GUY! BE A PAL! JUST THIS ONCE.
I WOULDN'T ASK IF IT WASN'T IMPORTANT.

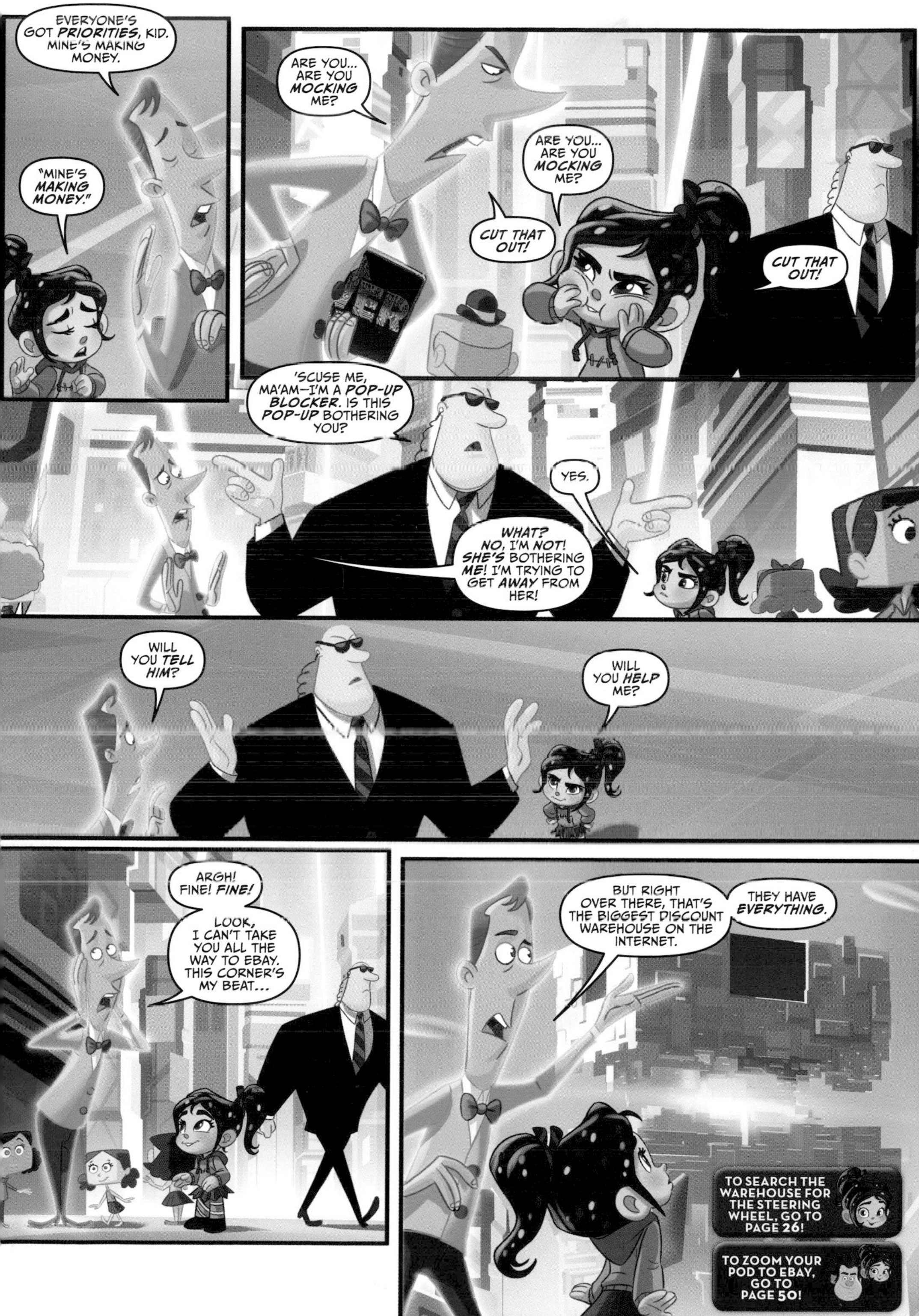
EVERYONE'S GOT PRIORITIES, KID. MINE'S MAKING MONEY.
"MINE'S MAKING MONEY."
ARE YOU... ARE YOU MOCKING ME?
ARE YOU... ARE YOU MOCKING ME?
CUT THAT OUT!
CUT THAT OUT!
'SCUSE ME, MA'AM—I'M A POP-UP BLOCKER. IS THIS POP-UP BOTHERING YOU?
YES.
WHAT? NO, I'M NOT! SHE'S BOTHERING ME! I'M TRYING TO GET AWAY FROM HER!
WILL YOU TELL HIM?
WILL YOU HELP ME?
ARGH! FINE! FINE!
LOOK, I CAN'T TAKE YOU ALL THE WAY TO EBAY. THIS CORNER'S MY BEAT...
BUT RIGHT OVER THERE, THAT'S THE BIGGEST DISCOUNT WAREHOUSE ON THE INTERNET.
THEY HAVE EVERYTHING.
TO SEARCH THE WAREHOUSE FOR THE STEERING WHEEL, GO TO PAGE 26!
TO ZOOM YOUR POD TO EBAY, GO TO PAGE 50!

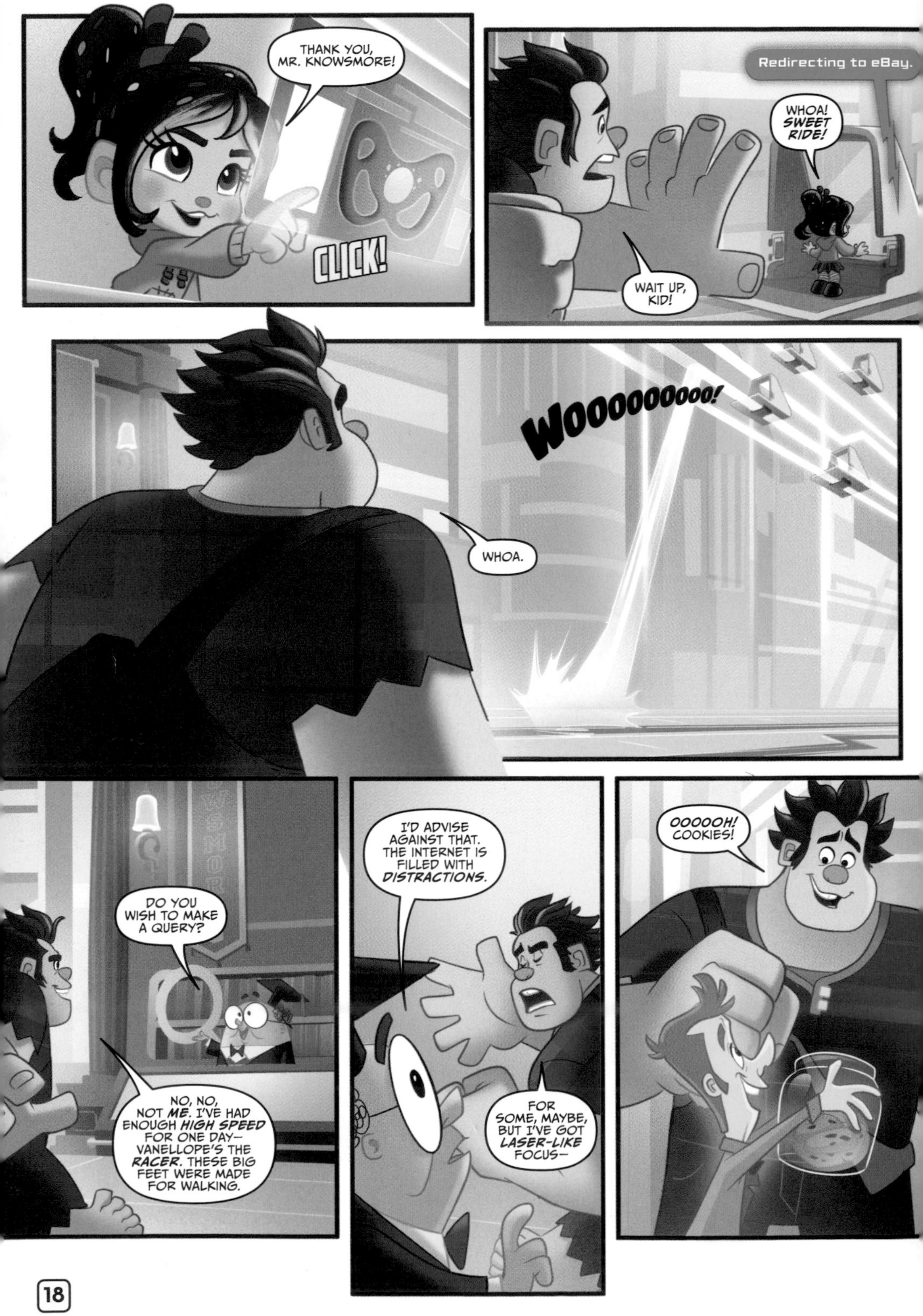
THANK YOU, MR. KNOWSMORE!
CLICK!
Redirecting to eBay.
WHOA! SWEET RIDE!
WAIT UP, KID!
WOOOOOOOOO!
WHOA.
DO YOU WISH TO MAKE A QUERY?
NO, NO, NOT ME. I'VE HAD ENOUGH HIGH SPEED FOR ONE DAY— VANELLOPE'S THE RACER. THESE BIG FEET WERE MADE FOR WALKING.
I'D ADVISE AGAINST THAT. THE INTERNET IS FILLED WITH DISTRACTIONS.
FOR SOME, MAYBE, BUT I'VE GOT LASER-LIKE FOCUS—
OOOOOH! COOKIES!

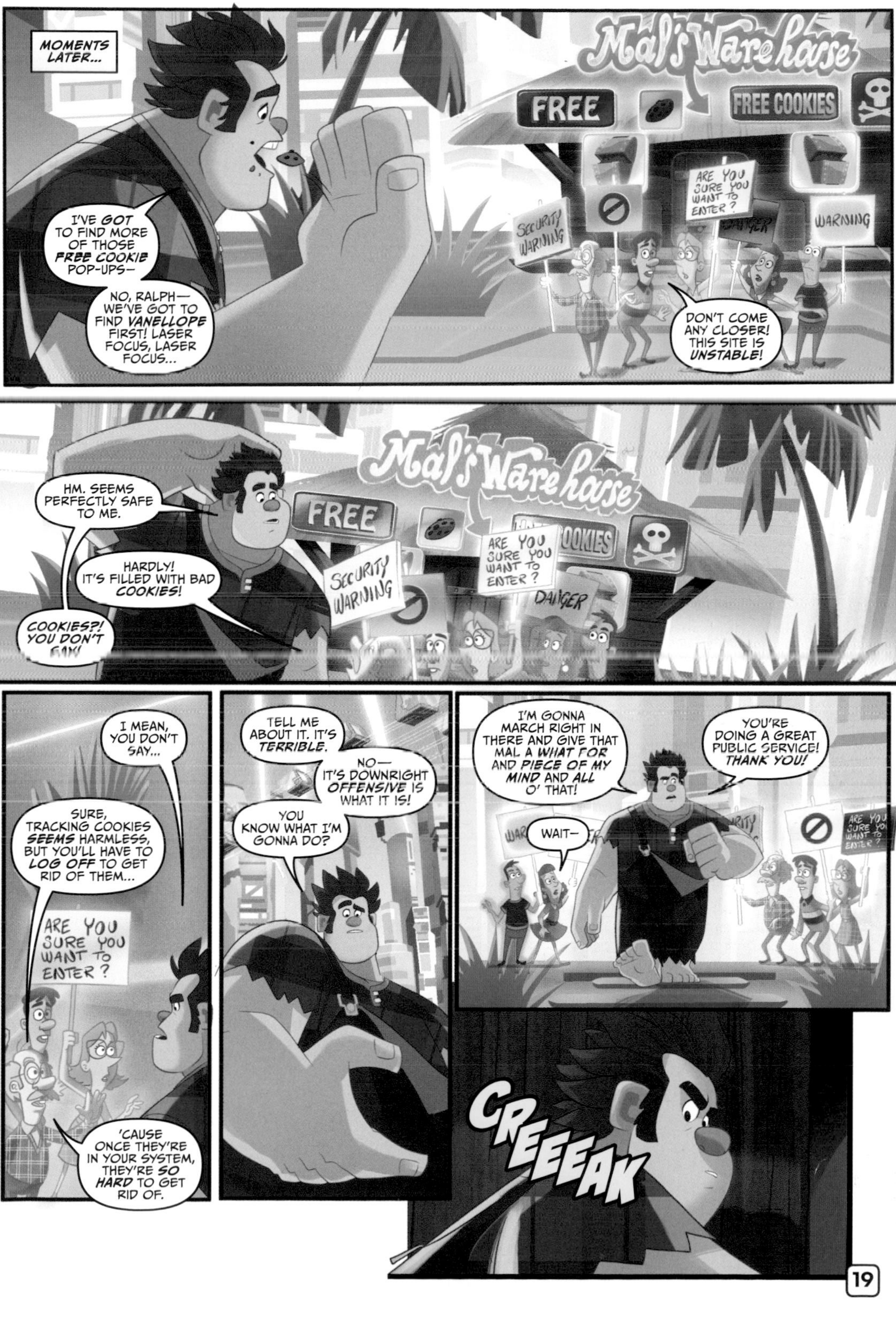
MOMENTS LATER...
Mal's Warehouse
FREE
FREE COOKIES
ARE YOU SURE YOU WANT TO ENTER?
SECURITY WARNING
DANGER
WARNING
I'VE *GOT* TO FIND MORE OF THOSE *FREE COOKIE* POP-UPS—
NO, RALPH— WE'VE GOT TO FIND *VANELLOPE* FIRST! LASER FOCUS, LASER FOCUS...
DON'T COME ANY CLOSER! THIS SITE IS *UNSTABLE!*
HM. SEEMS PERFECTLY SAFE TO ME.
HARDLY! IT'S FILLED WITH BAD *COOKIES!*
COOKIES?! YOU DON'T
I MEAN, YOU DON'T SAY...
SURE, TRACKING COOKIES *SEEMS* HARMLESS, BUT YOU'LL HAVE TO *LOG OFF* TO GET RID OF THEM...
'CAUSE ONCE THEY'RE IN YOUR SYSTEM, THEY'RE *SO HARD* TO GET RID OF.
TELL ME ABOUT IT. IT'S *TERRIBLE.*
NO— IT'S DOWNRIGHT *OFFENSIVE* IS WHAT IT IS!
YOU KNOW WHAT I'M GONNA DO?
I'M GONNA MARCH RIGHT IN THERE AND GIVE THAT MAL A *WHAT FOR* AND *PIECE OF MY MIND* AND *ALL* O' THAT!
YOU'RE DOING A GREAT PUBLIC SERVICE! *THANK YOU!*
WAIT—
CREEEAK

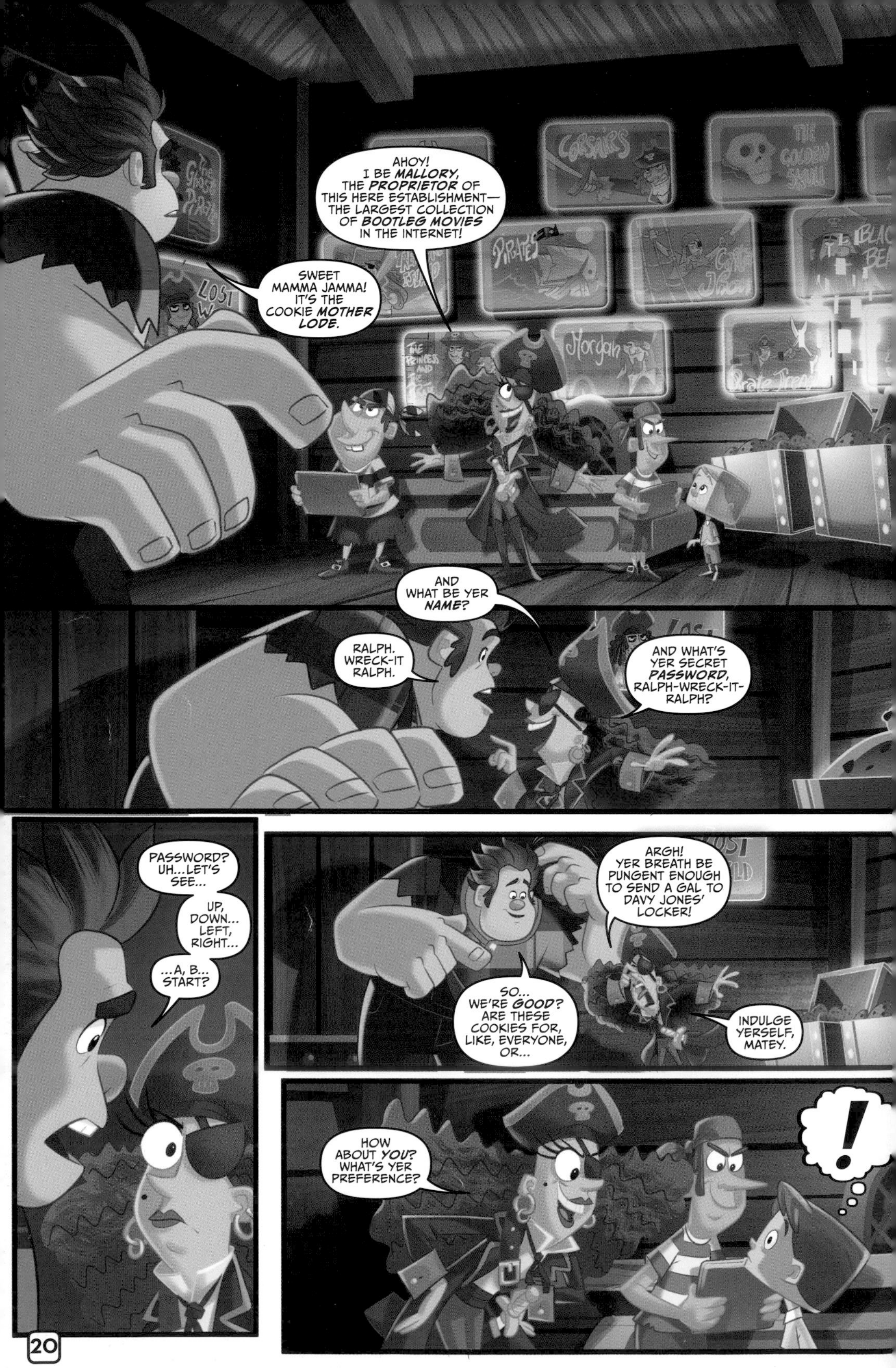
AHOY! I BE MALLORY, THE PROPRIETOR OF THIS HERE ESTABLISHMENT— THE LARGEST COLLECTION OF BOOTLEG MOVIES IN THE INTERNET!
SWEET MAMMA JAMMA! IT'S THE COOKIE MOTHER LODE.
CORSAIRS
THE GOLDEN SKULL
PIRATES
MORGAN
AND WHAT BE YER NAME?
RALPH. WRECK-IT RALPH.
AND WHAT'S YER SECRET PASSWORD, RALPH-WRECK-IT-RALPH?
PASSWORD? UH...LET'S SEE...
UP, DOWN... LEFT, RIGHT...
...A, B... START?
ARGH! YER BREATH BE PUNGENT ENOUGH TO SEND A GAL TO DAVY JONES' LOCKER!
SO... WE'RE GOOD? ARE THESE COOKIES FOR, LIKE, EVERYONE, OR...
INDULGE YERSELF, MATEY.
HOW ABOUT YOU? WHAT'S YER PREFERENCE?
!

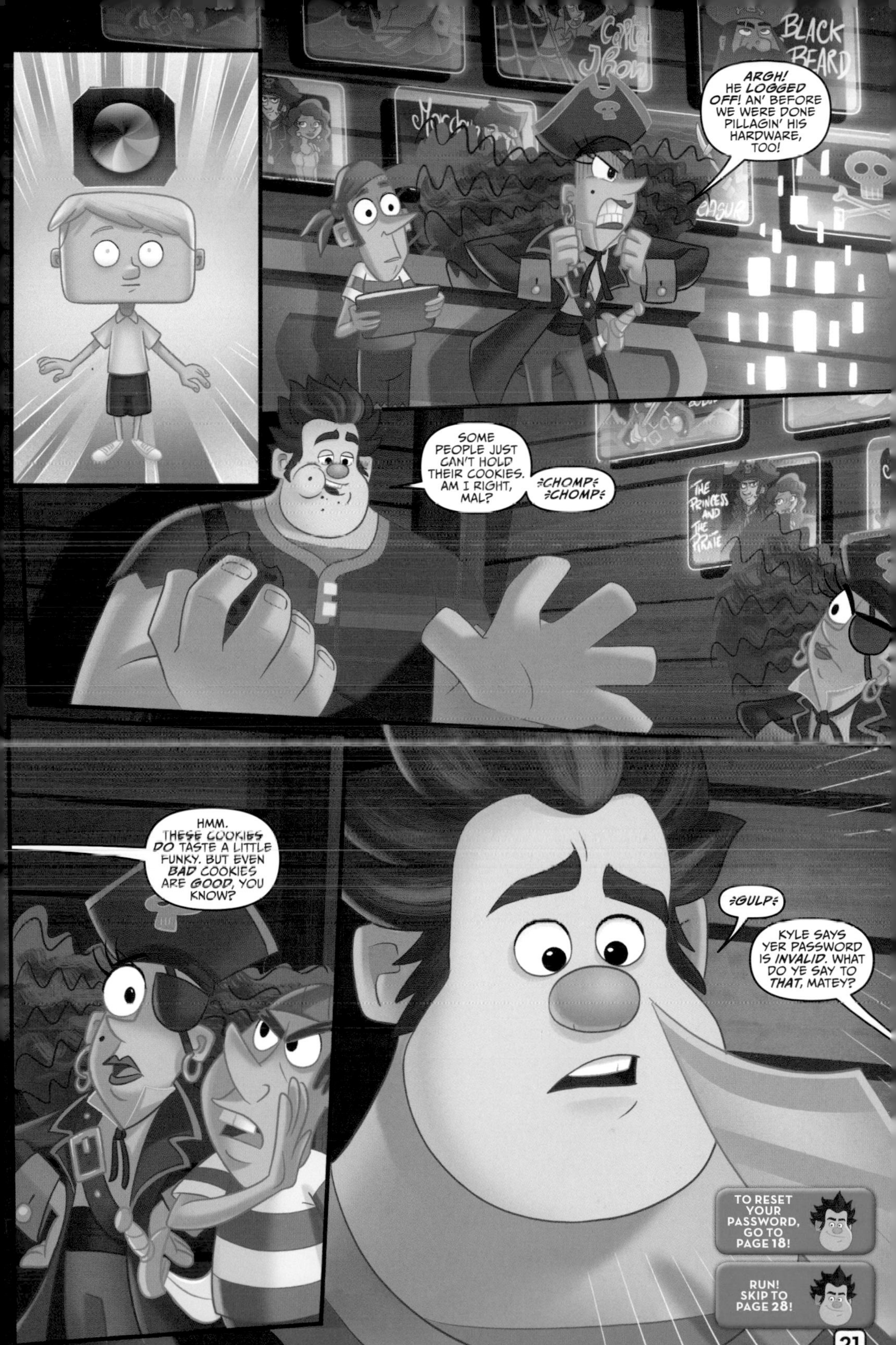
BLACK BEARD
ARGH! HE LOGGED OFF! AN' BEFORE WE WERE DONE PILLAGIN' HIS HARDWARE, TOO!
SOME PEOPLE JUST CAN'T HOLD THEIR COOKIES. AM I RIGHT, MAL?
CHOMP CHOMP
THE PRINCESS AND THE PIRATE
HMM. THESE COOKIES DO TASTE A LITTLE FUNKY. BUT EVEN BAD COOKIES ARE GOOD, YOU KNOW?
GULP
KYLE SAYS YER PASSWORD IS INVALID. WHAT DO YE SAY TO THAT, MATEY?

TO RESET YOUR PASSWORD, GO TO PAGE 18!

RUN! SKIP TO PAGE 28!

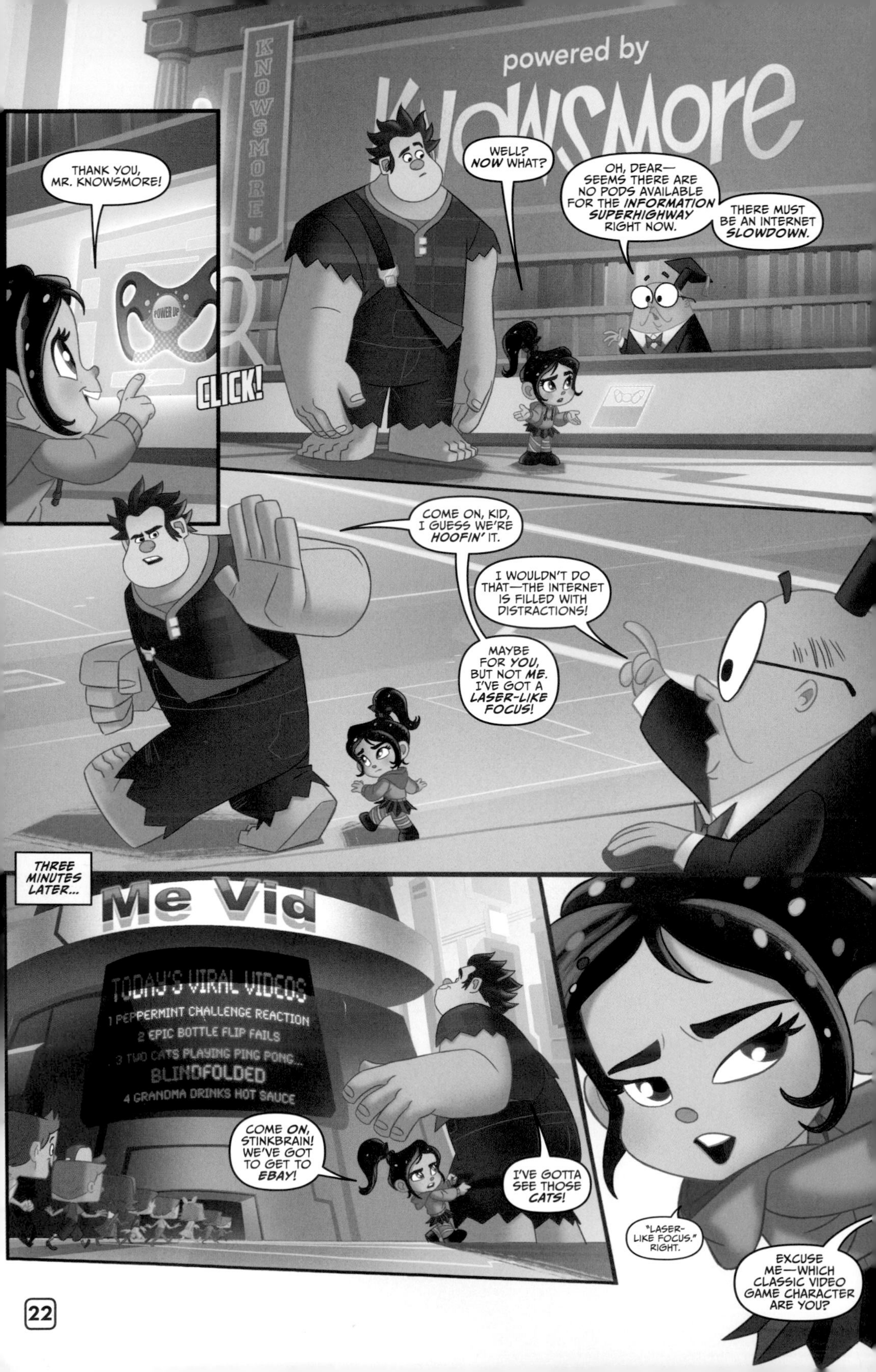
powered by
KNOWSMORE
KNOWSMORE
THANK YOU, MR. KNOWSMORE!
POWER UP
CLICK!
WELL? NOW WHAT?
OH, DEAR— SEEMS THERE ARE NO PODS AVAILABLE FOR THE INFORMATION SUPERHIGHWAY RIGHT NOW.
THERE MUST BE AN INTERNET SLOWDOWN.
COME ON, KID, I GUESS WE'RE HOOFIN' IT.
I WOULDN'T DO THAT—THE INTERNET IS FILLED WITH DISTRACTIONS!
MAYBE FOR YOU, BUT NOT ME. I'VE GOT A LASER-LIKE FOCUS!
THREE MINUTES LATER...
Me Vid
TODAY'S VIRAL VIDEOS
1 PEPPERMINT CHALLENGE REACTION
2 EPIC BOTTLE FLIP FAILS
3 TWO CATS PLAYING PING PONG... BLINDFOLDED
4 GRANDMA DRINKS HOT SAUCE
COME ON, STINKBRAIN! WE'VE GOT TO GET TO EBAY!
I'VE GOTTA SEE THOSE CATS!
"LASER-LIKE FOCUS." RIGHT.
EXCUSE ME—WHICH CLASSIC VIDEO GAME CHARACTER ARE YOU?

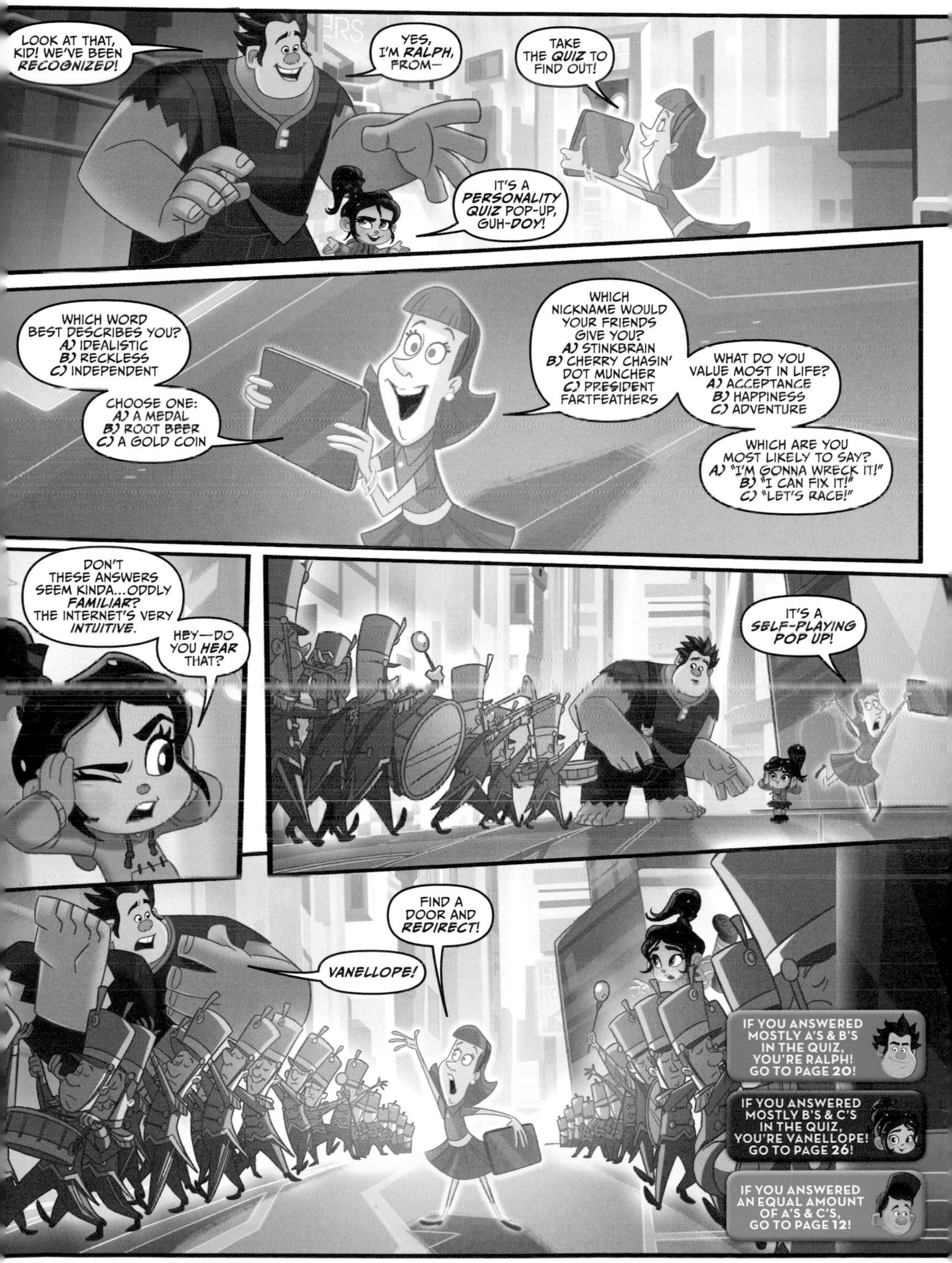

LOOK AT THAT, KID! WE'VE BEEN RECOGNIZED!
YES, I'M RALPH, FROM—
TAKE THE QUIZ TO FIND OUT!
IT'S A PERSONALITY QUIZ POP-UP, GUH-DOY!
WHICH WORD BEST DESCRIBES YOU? A) IDEALISTIC B) RECKLESS C) INDEPENDENT
CHOOSE ONE: A) A MEDAL B) ROOT BEER C) A GOLD COIN
WHICH NICKNAME WOULD YOUR FRIENDS GIVE YOU? A) STINKBRAIN B) CHERRY CHASIN' DOT MUNCHER C) PRESIDENT FARTFEATHERS
WHAT DO YOU VALUE MOST IN LIFE? A) ACCEPTANCE B) HAPPINESS C) ADVENTURE
WHICH ARE YOU MOST LIKELY TO SAY? A) "I'M GONNA WRECK IT!" B) "I CAN FIX IT!" C) "LET'S RACE!"
DON'T THESE ANSWERS SEEM KINDA...ODDLY FAMILIAR? THE INTERNET'S VERY INTUITIVE.
HEY—DO YOU HEAR THAT?
IT'S A SELF-PLAYING POP UP!
FIND A DOOR AND REDIRECT!
VANELLOPE!
IF YOU ANSWERED MOSTLY A'S & B'S IN THE QUIZ, YOU'RE RALPH! GO TO PAGE 20!
IF YOU ANSWERED MOSTLY B'S & C'S IN THE QUIZ, YOU'RE VANELLOPE! GO TO PAGE 26!
IF YOU ANSWERED AN EQUAL AMOUNT OF A'S & C'S, GO TO PAGE 12!

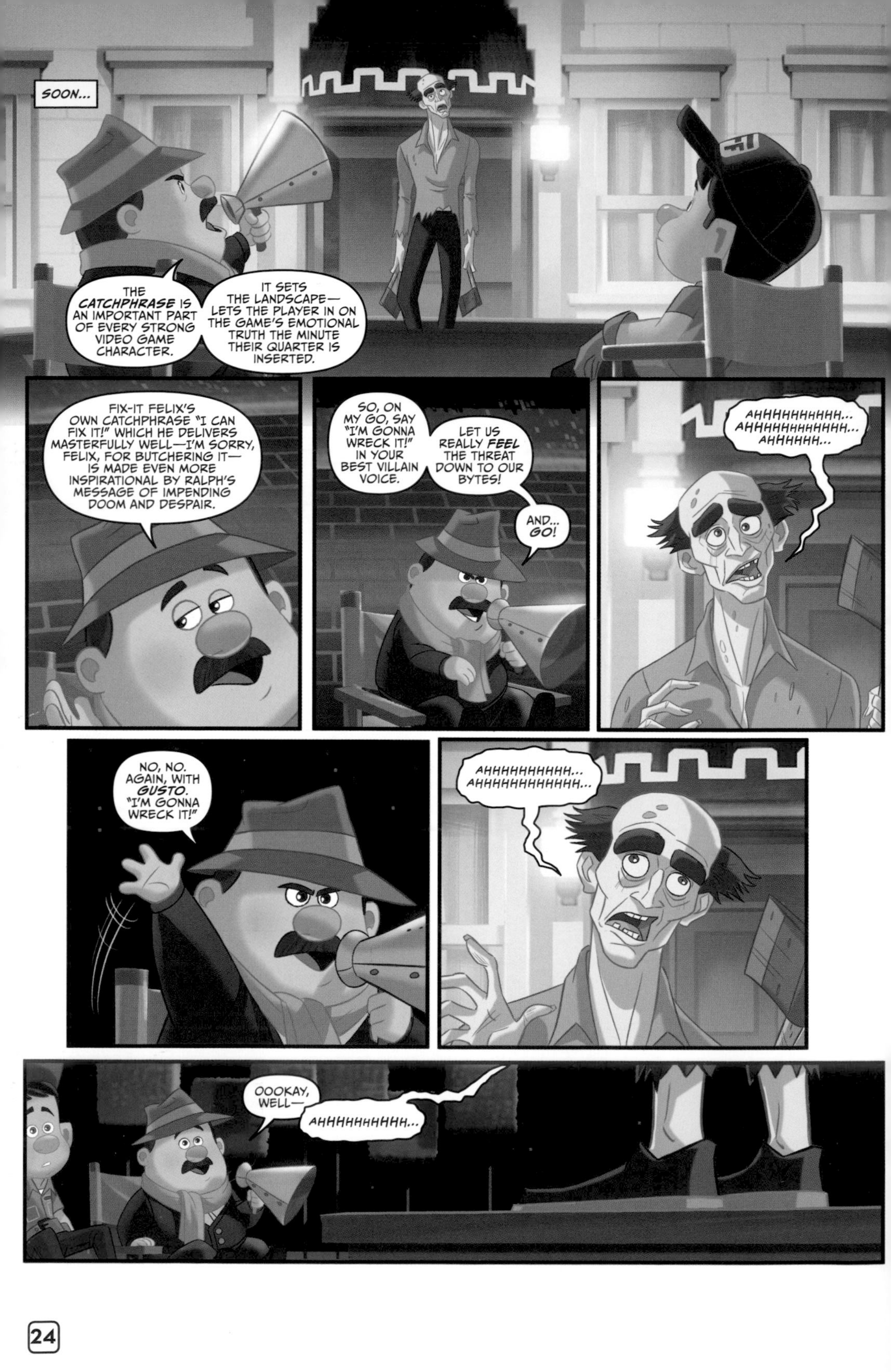
SOON...
THE CATCHPHRASE IS AN IMPORTANT PART OF EVERY STRONG VIDEO GAME CHARACTER.
IT SETS THE LANDSCAPE— LETS THE PLAYER IN ON THE GAME'S EMOTIONAL TRUTH THE MINUTE THEIR QUARTER IS INSERTED.
FIX-IT FELIX'S OWN CATCHPHRASE "I CAN FIX IT!" WHICH HE DELIVERS MASTERFULLY WELL—I'M SORRY, FELIX, FOR BUTCHERING IT— IS MADE EVEN MORE INSPIRATIONAL BY RALPH'S MESSAGE OF IMPENDING DOOM AND DESPAIR.
SO, ON MY GO, SAY "I'M GONNA WRECK IT!" IN YOUR BEST VILLAIN VOICE.
LET US REALLY FEEL THE THREAT DOWN TO OUR BYTES!
AND... GO!
AHHHHHHHHHH... AHHHHHHHHHHHH... AHHHHHH...
NO, NO. AGAIN, WITH GUSTO. "I'M GONNA WRECK IT!"
AHHHHHHHHHH... AHHHHHHHHHHHH...
OOOKAY, WELL—
AHHHHHHHHHH...

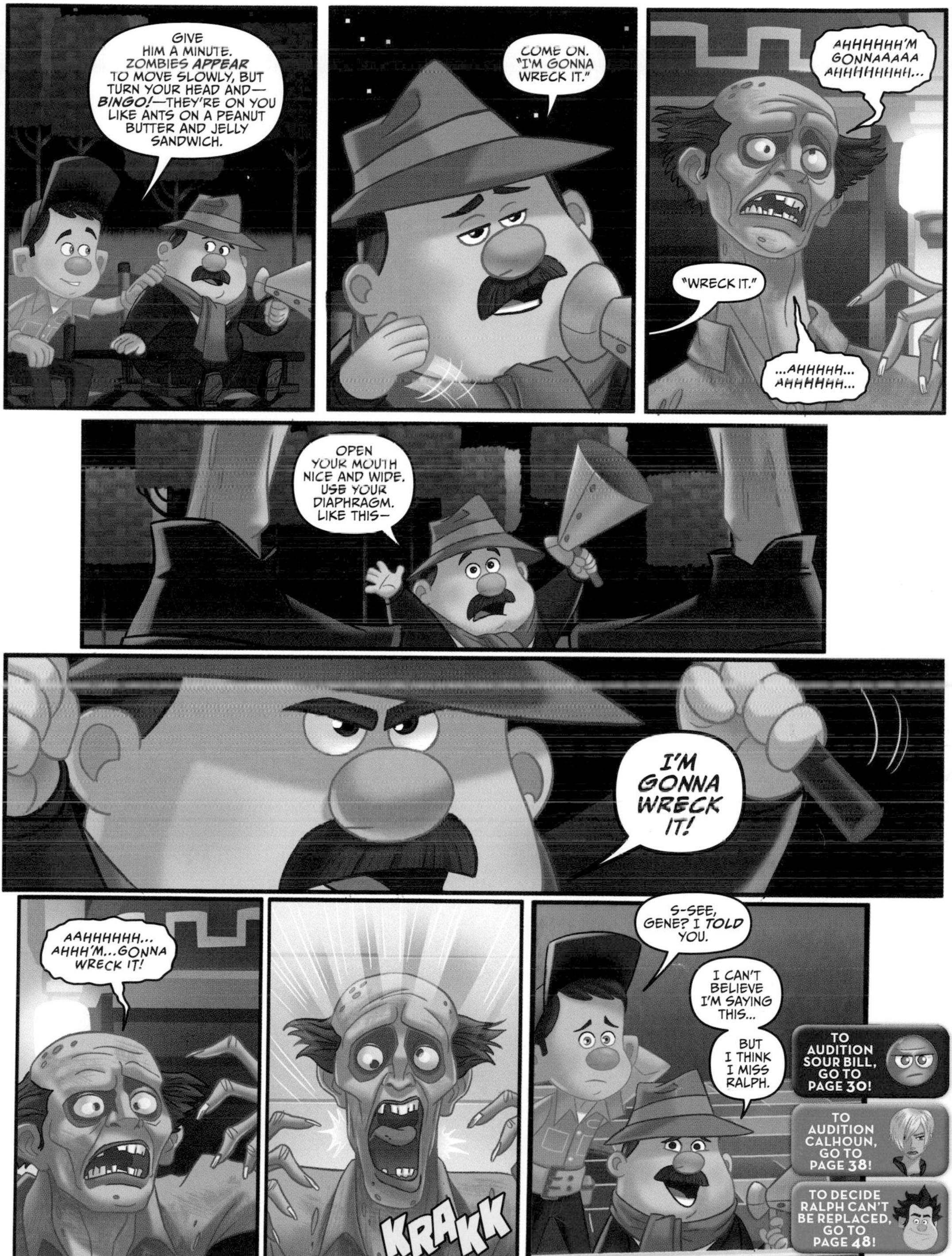

GIVE HIM A MINUTE. ZOMBIES APPEAR TO MOVE SLOWLY, BUT TURN YOUR HEAD AND—BINGO!—THEY'RE ON YOU LIKE ANTS ON A PEANUT BUTTER AND JELLY SANDWICH.
COME ON. "I'M GONNA WRECK IT."
AHHHHHH'M GONNAAAAA AHHHHHHHH...
"WRECK IT."
...AHHHHH... AHHHHHH...
OPEN YOUR MOUTH NICE AND WIDE. USE YOUR DIAPHRAGM. LIKE THIS—
I'M GONNA WRECK IT!
AAHHHHHH... AHHH'M...GONNA WRECK IT!
KRAKK
S-SEE, GENE? I TOLD YOU.
I CAN'T BELIEVE I'M SAYING THIS...
BUT I THINK I MISS RALPH.

TO AUDITION SOUR BILL, GO TO PAGE 30!

TO AUDITION CALHOUN, GO TO PAGE 38!

TO DECIDE RALPH CAN'T BE REPLACED, GO TO PAGE 48!

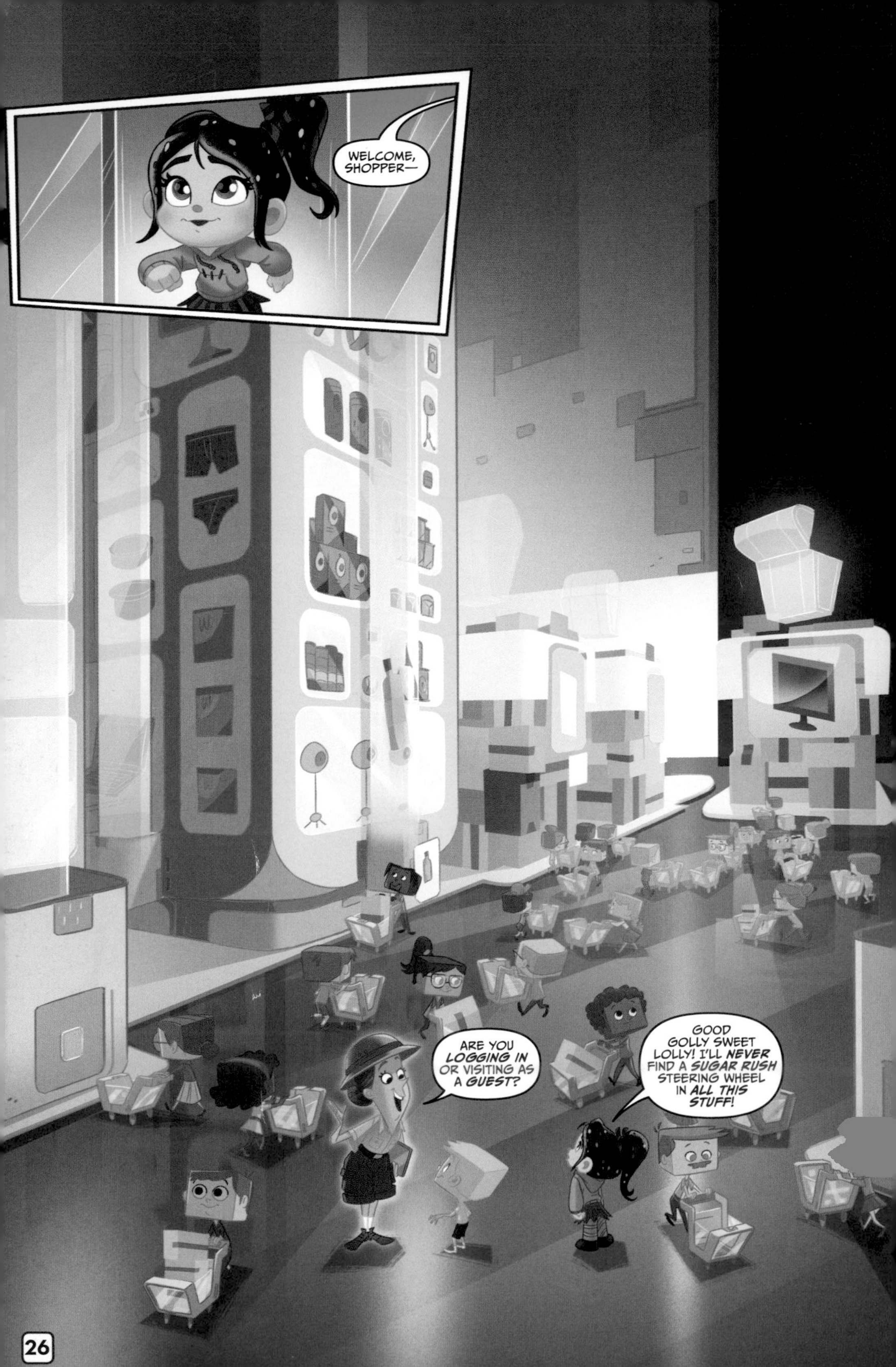
WELCOME, SHOPPER—
ARE YOU LOGGING IN OR VISITING AS A GUEST?
GOOD GOLLY SWEET LOLLY! I'LL NEVER FIND A SUGAR RUSH STEERING WHEEL IN ALL THIS STUFF!

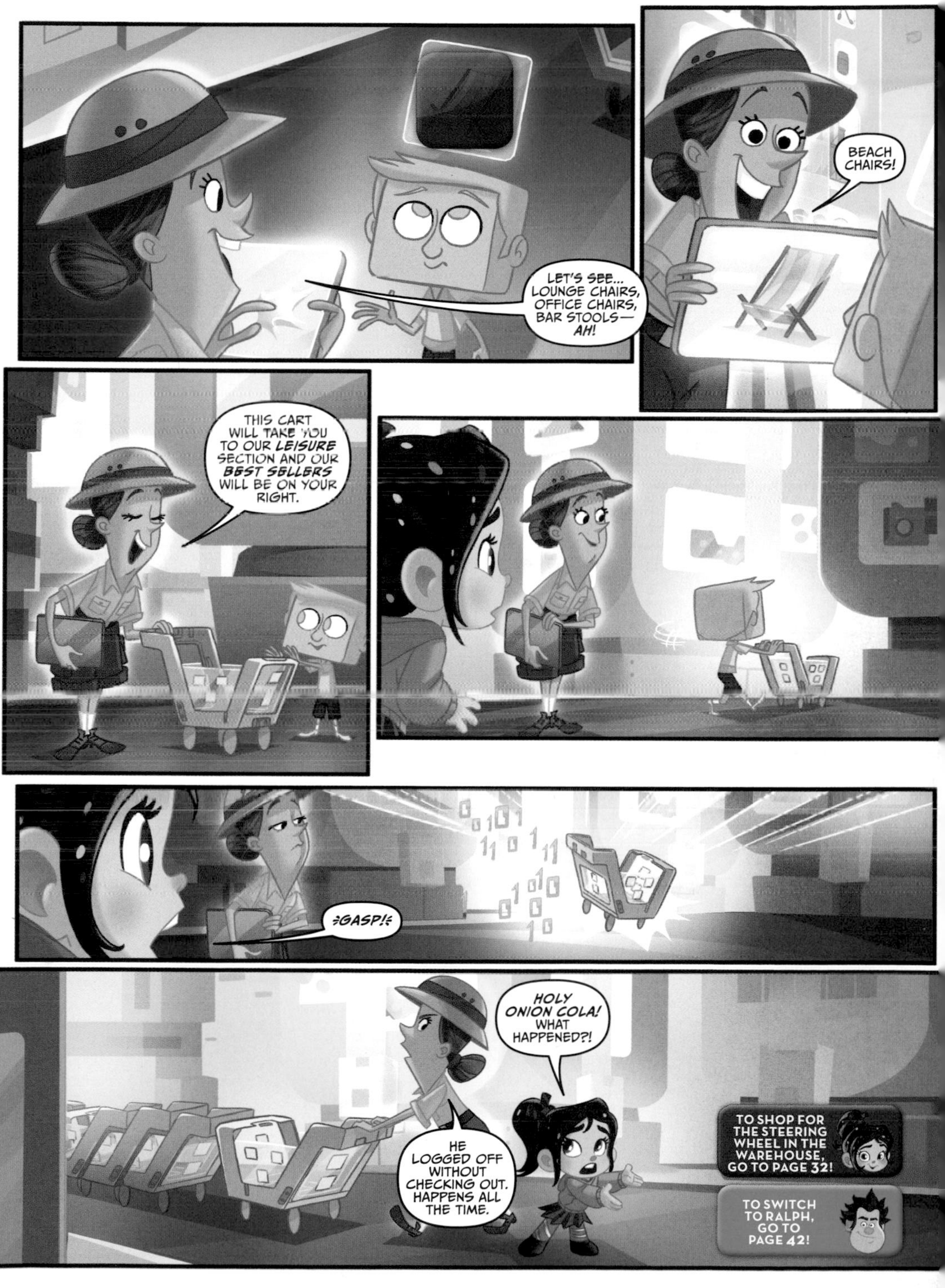

LET'S SEE... LOUNGE CHAIRS, OFFICE CHAIRS, BAR STOOLS— AH!
BEACH CHAIRS!
THIS CART WILL TAKE YOU TO OUR LEISURE SECTION AND OUR BEST SELLERS WILL BE ON YOUR RIGHT.
GASP!
HOLY ONION COLA! WHAT HAPPENED?!
HE LOGGED OFF WITHOUT CHECKING OUT. HAPPENS ALL THE TIME.
TO SHOP FOR THE STEERING WHEEL IN THE WAREHOUSE, GO TO PAGE 32!
TO SWITCH TO RALPH, GO TO PAGE 42!

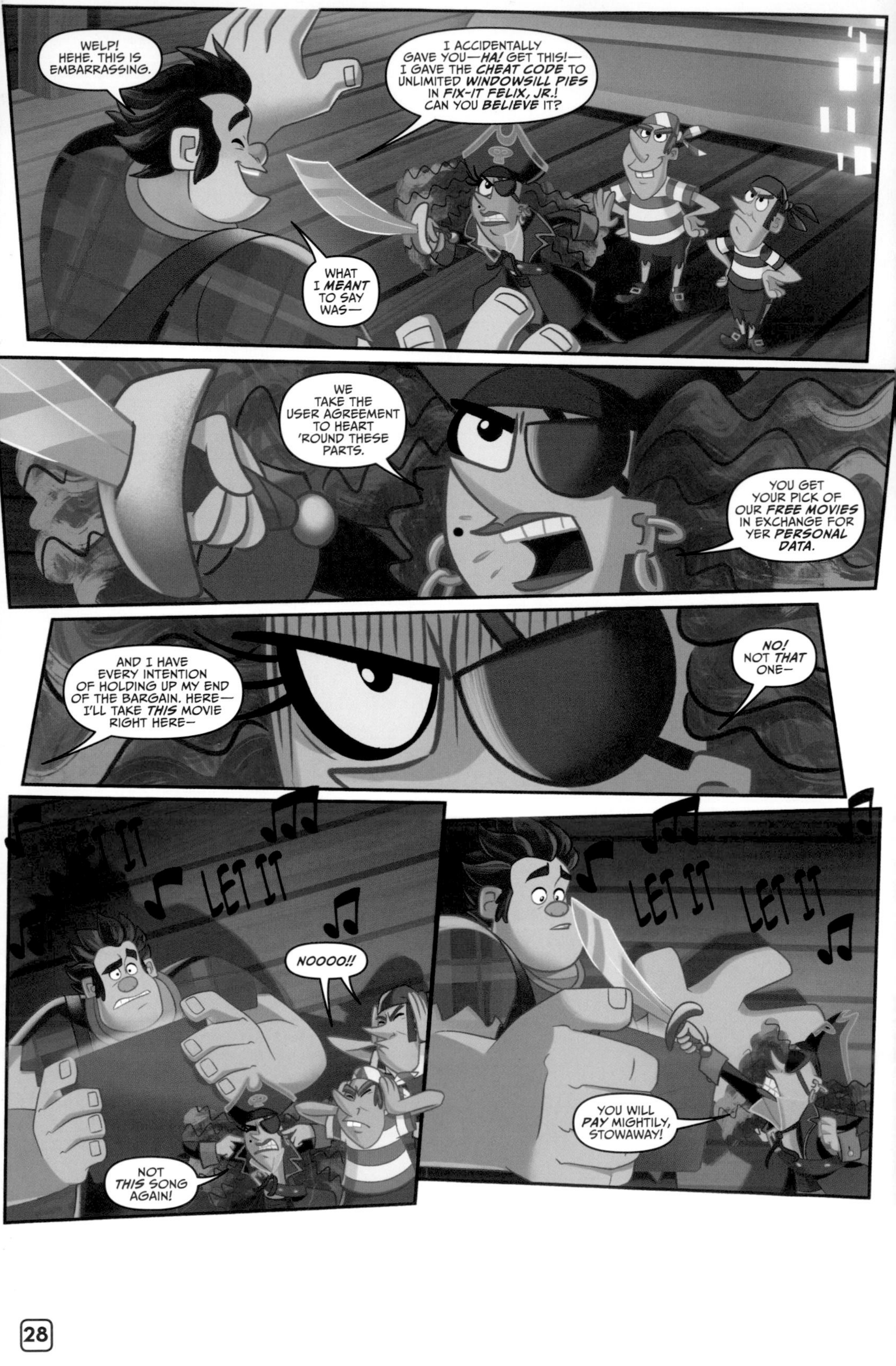
WELP! HEHE. THIS IS EMBARRASSING.
I ACCIDENTALLY GAVE YOU—HA! GET THIS!—I GAVE THE CHEAT CODE TO UNLIMITED WINDOWSILL PIES IN FIX-IT FELIX, JR.! CAN YOU BELIEVE IT?
WHAT I MEANT TO SAY WAS—
WE TAKE THE USER AGREEMENT TO HEART 'ROUND THESE PARTS.
YOU GET YOUR PICK OF OUR FREE MOVIES IN EXCHANGE FOR YER PERSONAL DATA.
AND I HAVE EVERY INTENTION OF HOLDING UP MY END OF THE BARGAIN. HERE—I'LL TAKE THIS MOVIE RIGHT HERE–
NO! NOT THAT ONE–
LET IT
LET IT
NOOOO!!
NOT THIS SONG AGAIN!
LET IT
LET IT
YOU WILL PAY MIGHTILY, STOWAWAY!

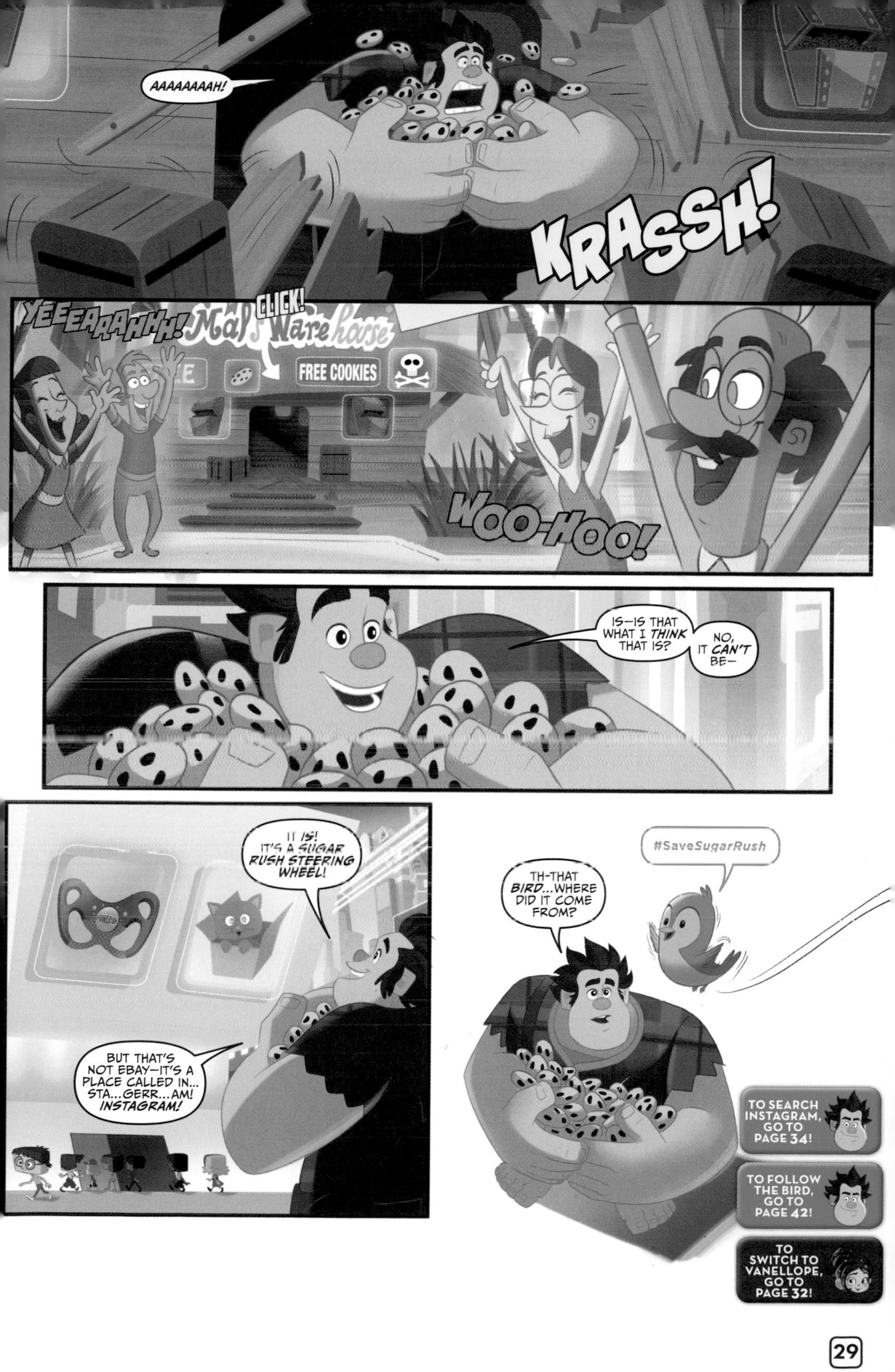
AAAAAAAAH!
KRASSH!
YEEEAAAAHHH!
CLICK!
FREE COOKIES
WOO-HOO!
IS—IS THAT WHAT I *THINK* THAT IS?
NO, IT *CAN'T* BE—
IT *IS*! IT'S A *SUGAR RUSH STEERING WHEEL!*
BUT THAT'S NOT EBAY—IT'S A PLACE CALLED IN... STA...GERR...AM! *INSTAGRAM!*
#SaveSugarRush
TH-THAT *BIRD*...WHERE DID IT COME FROM?

TO SEARCH INSTAGRAM, GO TO PAGE 34!
TO FOLLOW THE BIRD, GO TO PAGE 42!
TO SWITCH TO VANELLOPE, GO TO PAGE 32!

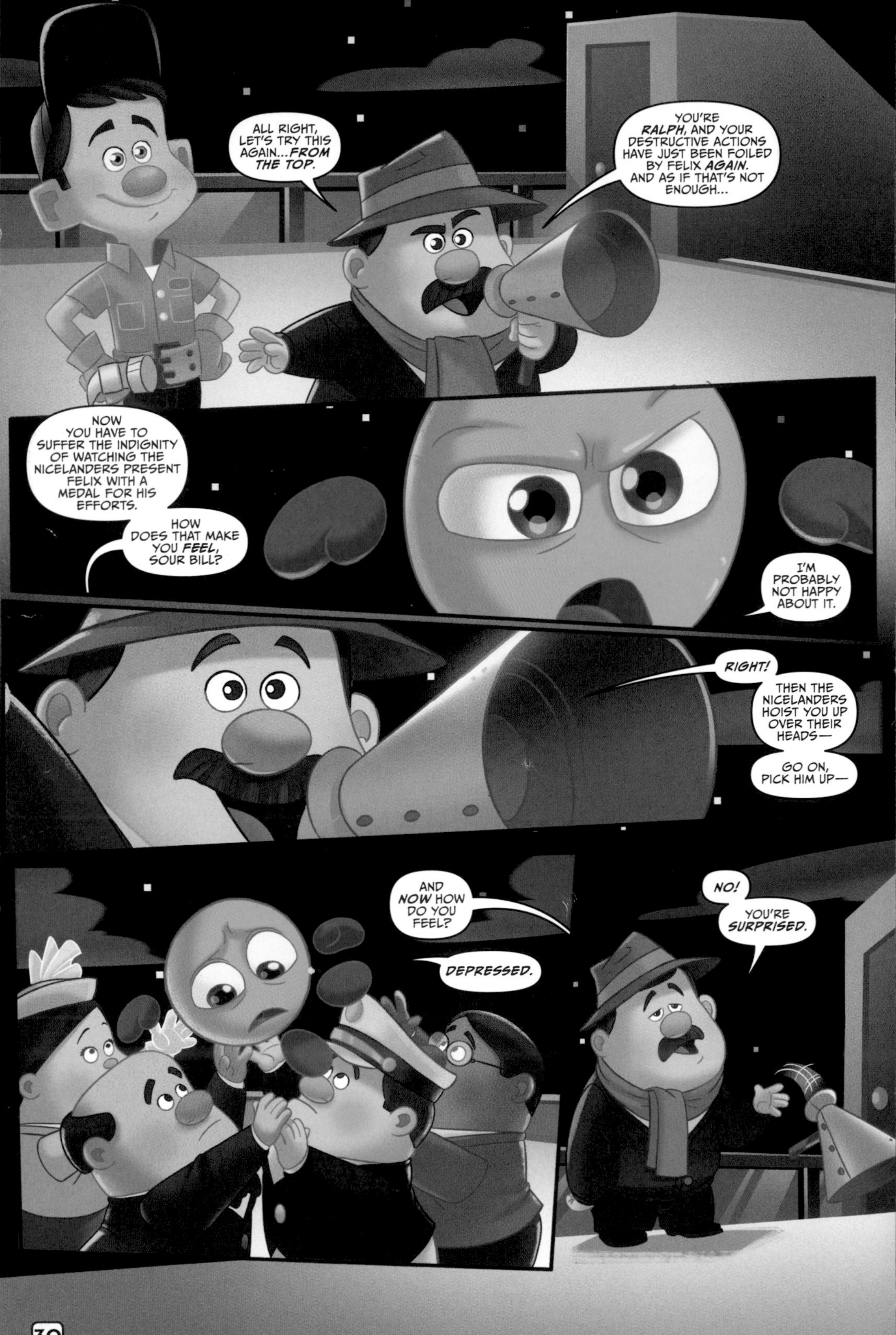
ALL RIGHT, LET'S TRY THIS AGAIN...FROM THE TOP.
YOU'RE RALPH, AND YOUR DESTRUCTIVE ACTIONS HAVE JUST BEEN FOILED BY FELIX AGAIN. AND AS IF THAT'S NOT ENOUGH...
NOW YOU HAVE TO SUFFER THE INDIGNITY OF WATCHING THE NICELANDERS PRESENT FELIX WITH A MEDAL FOR HIS EFFORTS.
HOW DOES THAT MAKE YOU FEEL, SOUR BILL?
I'M PROBABLY NOT HAPPY ABOUT IT.
RIGHT!
THEN THE NICELANDERS HOIST YOU UP OVER THEIR HEADS—
GO ON, PICK HIM UP—
AND NOW HOW DO YOU FEEL?
DEPRESSED.
NO!
YOU'RE SURPRISED.

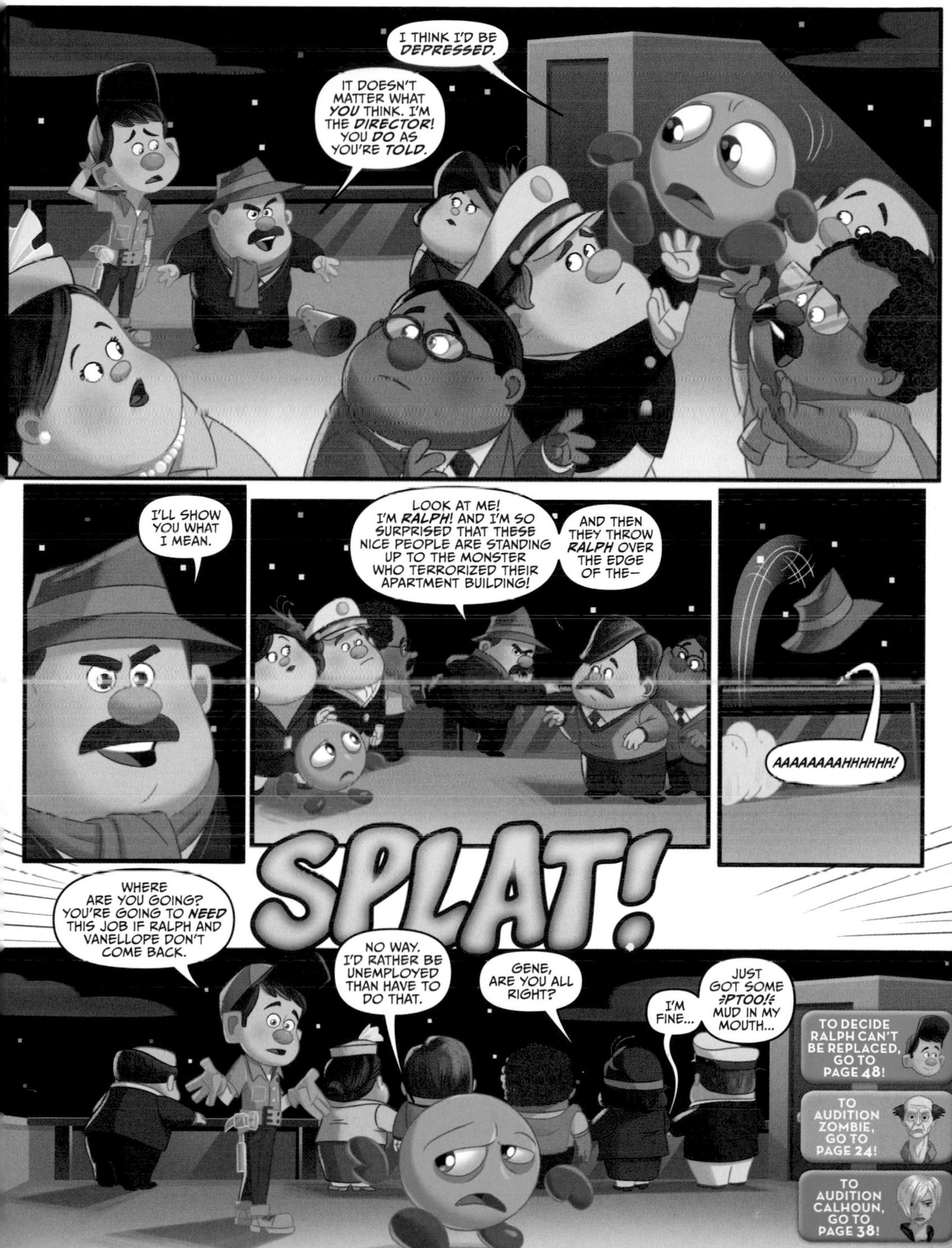

I THINK I'D BE DEPRESSED.
IT DOESN'T MATTER WHAT YOU THINK. I'M THE DIRECTOR! YOU DO AS YOU'RE TOLD.
I'LL SHOW YOU WHAT I MEAN.
LOOK AT ME! I'M RALPH! AND I'M SO SURPRISED THAT THESE NICE PEOPLE ARE STANDING UP TO THE MONSTER WHO TERRORIZED THEIR APARTMENT BUILDING!
AND THEN THEY THROW RALPH OVER THE EDGE OF THE—
AAAAAAAAHHHHHH!
SPLAT!
WHERE ARE YOU GOING? YOU'RE GOING TO NEED THIS JOB IF RALPH AND VANELLOPE DON'T COME BACK.
NO WAY. I'D RATHER BE UNEMPLOYED THAN HAVE TO DO THAT.
GENE, ARE YOU ALL RIGHT?
I'M FINE...
JUST GOT SOME PTOO! MUD IN MY MOUTH...

TO DECIDE RALPH CAN'T BE REPLACED, GO TO PAGE 48!
TO AUDITION ZOMBIE, GO TO PAGE 24!
TO AUDITION CALHOUN, GO TO PAGE 38!

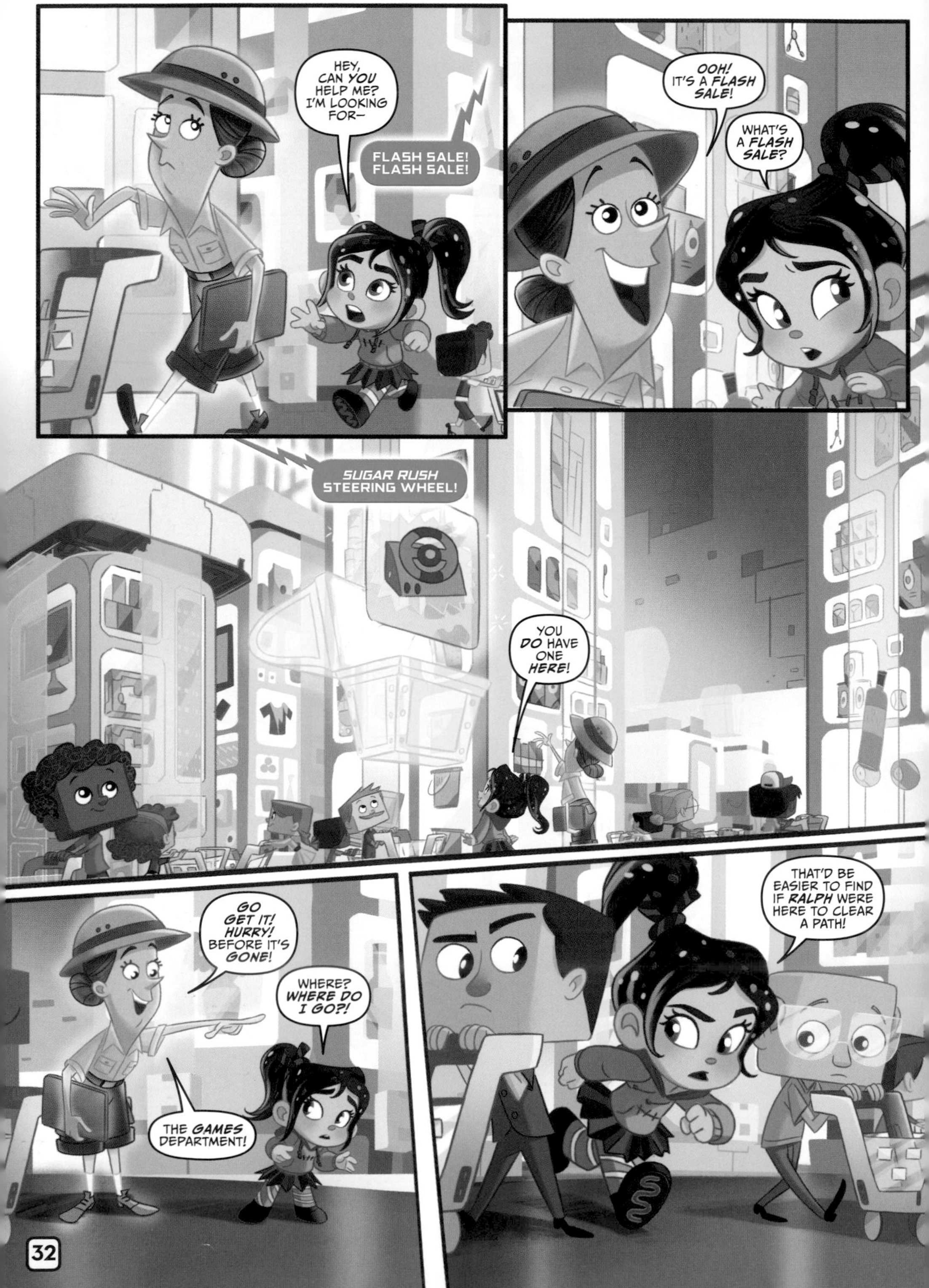
HEY, CAN YOU HELP ME? I'M LOOKING FOR—
FLASH SALE! FLASH SALE!
OOH! IT'S A FLASH SALE!
WHAT'S A FLASH SALE?
SUGAR RUSH STEERING WHEEL!
YOU DO HAVE ONE HERE!
GO GET IT! HURRY! BEFORE IT'S GONE!
WHERE? WHERE DO I GO?!
THE GAMES DEPARTMENT!
THAT'D BE EASIER TO FIND IF RALPH WERE HERE TO CLEAR A PATH!

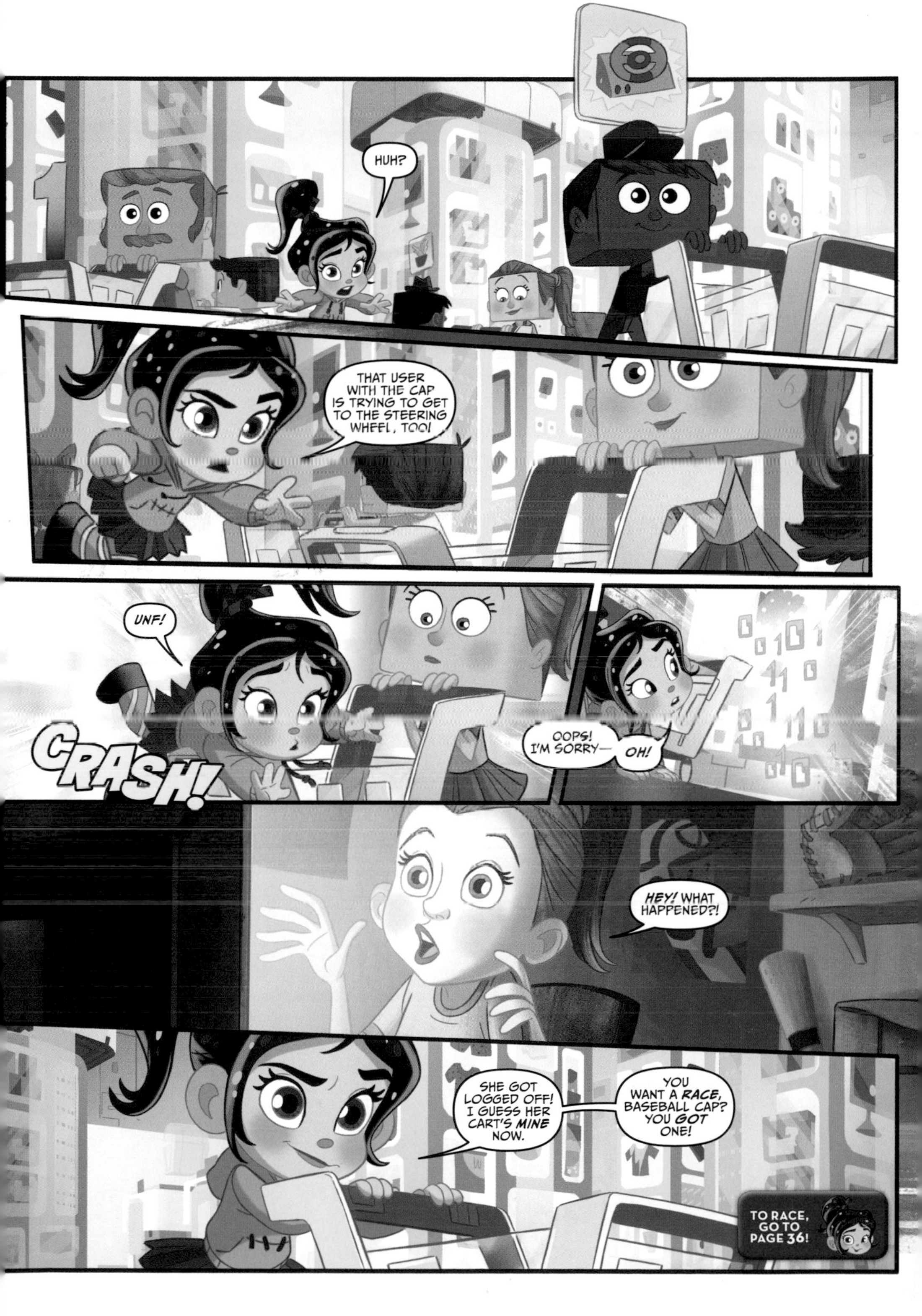

HUH?
THAT USER WITH THE CAP IS TRYING TO GET TO THE STEERING WHEEL, TOO!
UNF!
CRASH!
OOPS! I'M SORRY—
OH!
HEY! WHAT HAPPENED?!
SHE GOT LOGGED OFF! I GUESS HER CART'S MINE NOW.
YOU WANT A RACE, BASEBALL CAP? YOU GOT ONE!
TO RACE, GO TO PAGE 36!

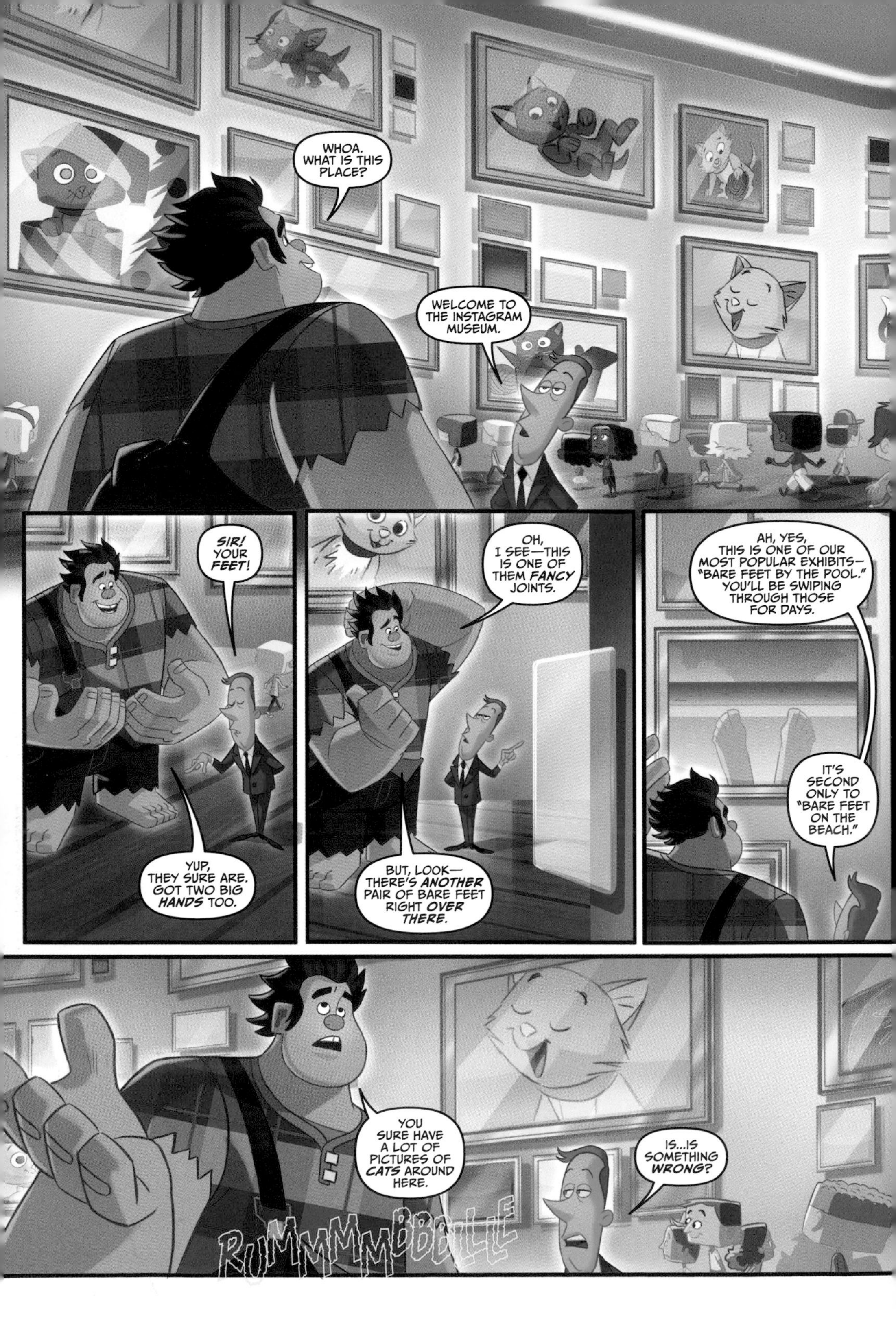
WHOA. WHAT IS THIS PLACE?
WELCOME TO THE INSTAGRAM MUSEUM.
SIR! YOUR FEET!
YUP, THEY SURE ARE. GOT TWO BIG HANDS TOO.
OH, I SEE—THIS IS ONE OF THEM FANCY JOINTS.
BUT, LOOK—THERE'S ANOTHER PAIR OF BARE FEET RIGHT OVER THERE.
AH, YES, THIS IS ONE OF OUR MOST POPULAR EXHIBITS—"BARE FEET BY THE POOL." YOU'LL BE SWIPING THROUGH THOSE FOR DAYS.
IT'S SECOND ONLY TO "BARE FEET ON THE BEACH."
YOU SURE HAVE A LOT OF PICTURES OF CATS AROUND HERE.
RUMMMMBBBLLE
IS...IS SOMETHING WRONG?

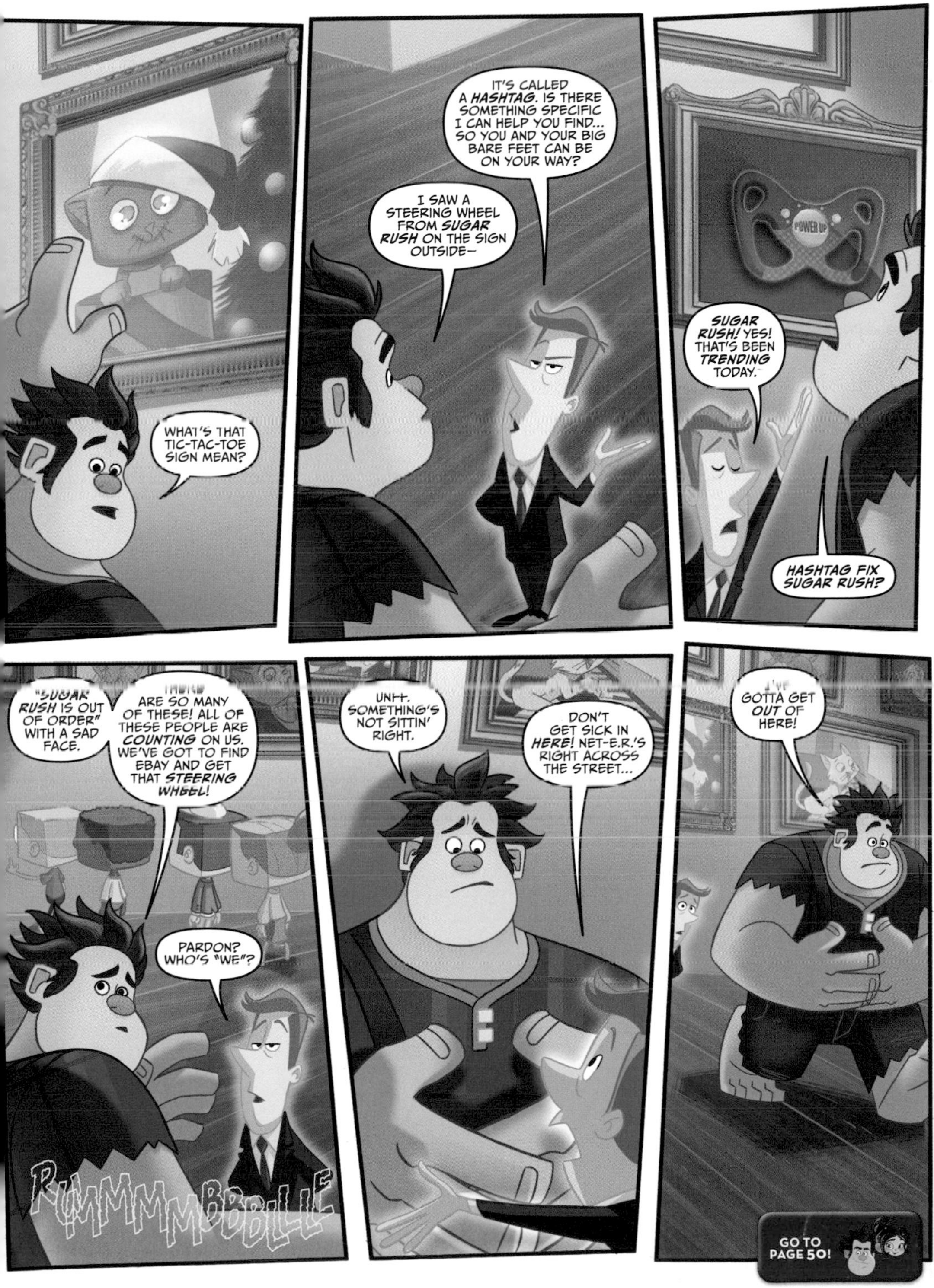
WHAT'S THAT TIC-TAC-TOE SIGN MEAN?
IT'S CALLED A HASHTAG. IS THERE SOMETHING SPECIFIC I CAN HELP YOU FIND... SO YOU AND YOUR BIG BARE FEET CAN BE ON YOUR WAY?
I SAW A STEERING WHEEL FROM SUGAR RUSH ON THE SIGN OUTSIDE–
POWER UP
SUGAR RUSH! YES! THAT'S BEEN TRENDING TODAY.
HASHTAG FIX SUGAR RUSH?
"SUGAR RUSH IS OUT OF ORDER" WITH A SAD FACE.
ARE SO MANY OF THESE! ALL OF THESE PEOPLE ARE COUNTING ON US. WE'VE GOT TO FIND EBAY AND GET THAT STEERING WHEEL!
PARDON? WHO'S "WE"?
RUMMMMBBBLLE
UNH. SOMETHING'S NOT SITTIN' RIGHT.
DON'T GET SICK IN HERE! NET-E.R.'S RIGHT ACROSS THE STREET...
GOTTA GET OUT OF HERE!

GO TO PAGE 50!

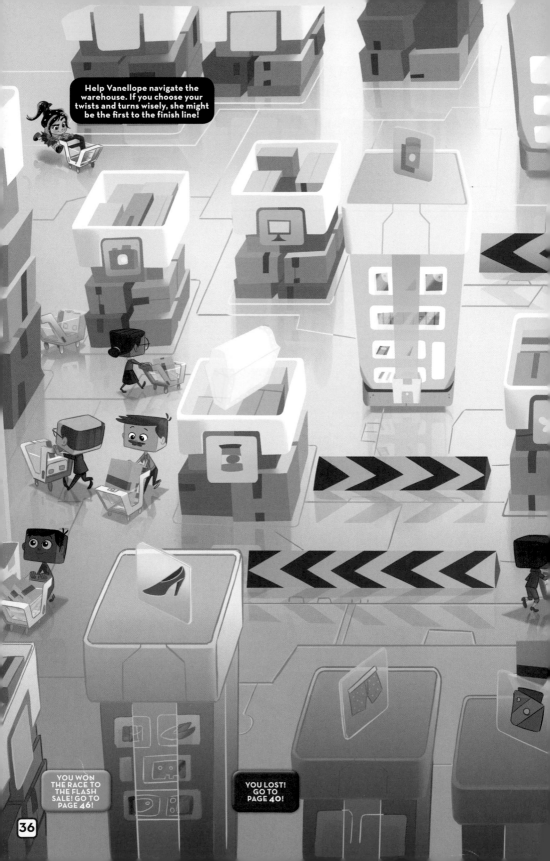

Help Vanellope navigate the warehouse. If you choose your twists and turns wisely, she might be the first to the finish line!

YOU WON THE RACE TO THE FLASH SALE! GO TO PAGE 46!

YOU LOST! GO TO PAGE 40!

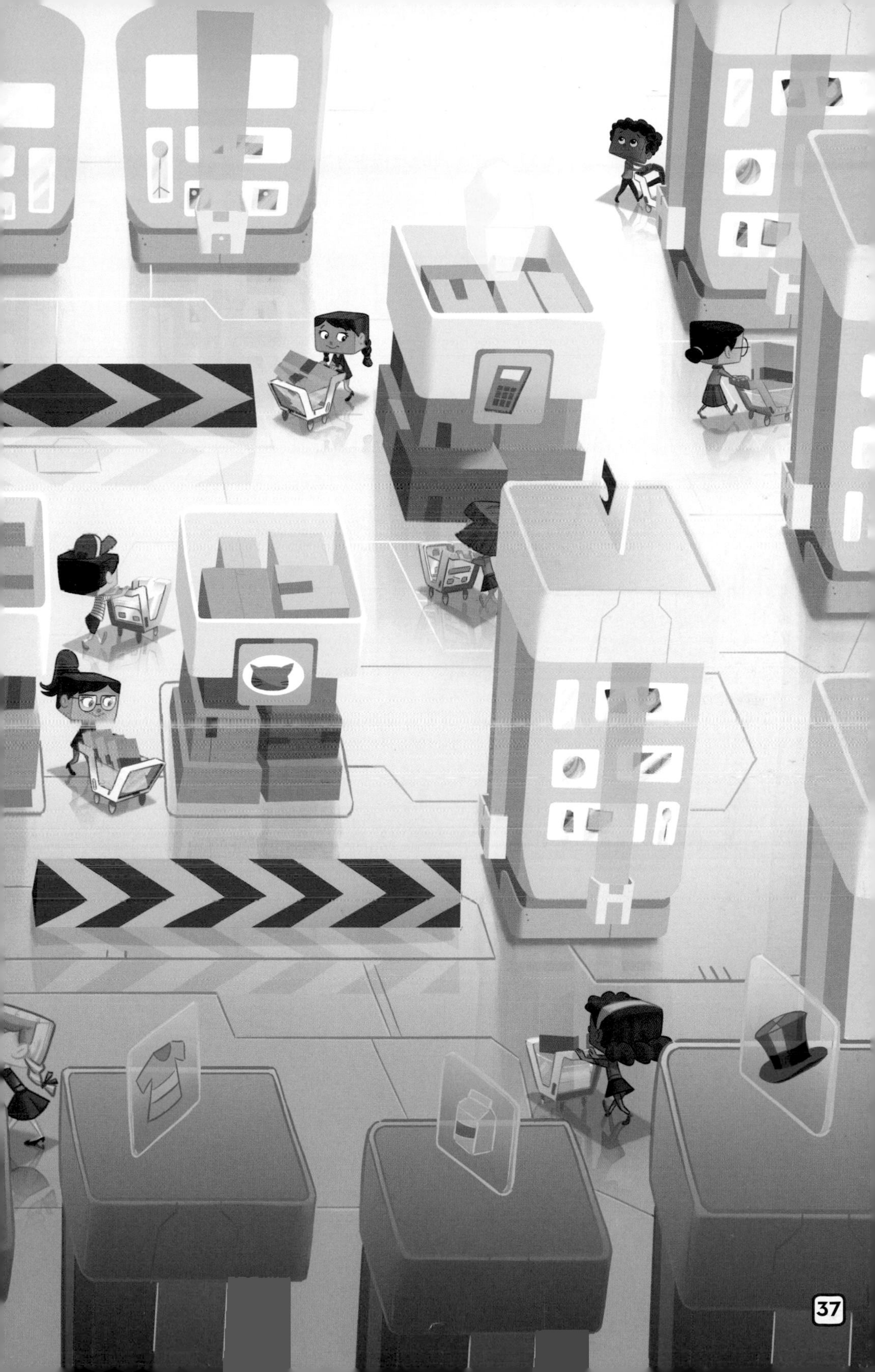

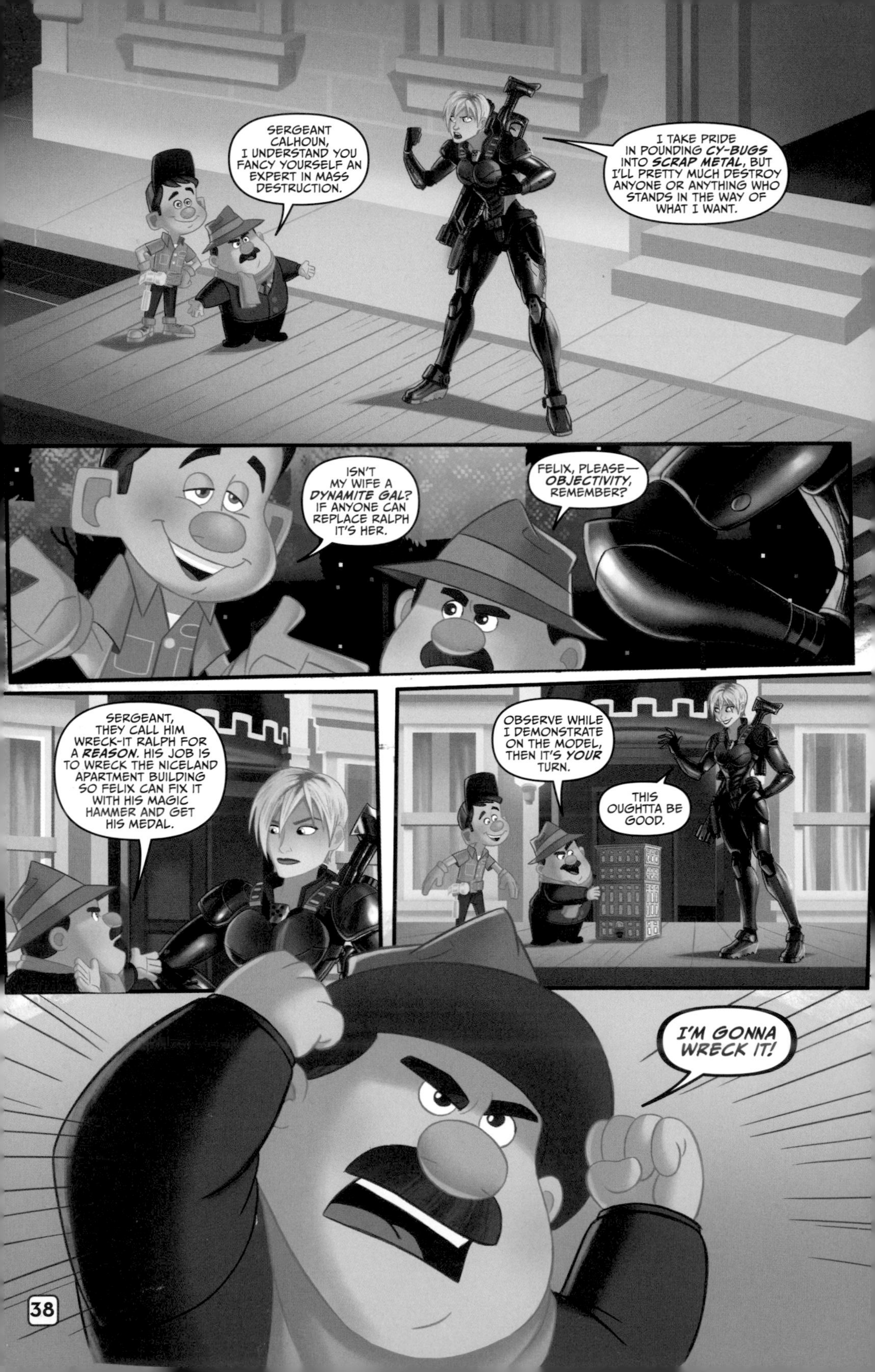
SERGEANT CALHOUN, I UNDERSTAND YOU FANCY YOURSELF AN EXPERT IN MASS DESTRUCTION.
I TAKE PRIDE IN POUNDING CY-BUGS INTO SCRAP METAL, BUT I'LL PRETTY MUCH DESTROY ANYONE OR ANYTHING WHO STANDS IN THE WAY OF WHAT I WANT.
ISN'T MY WIFE A DYNAMITE GAL? IF ANYONE CAN REPLACE RALPH IT'S HER.
FELIX, PLEASE— OBJECTIVITY, REMEMBER?
SERGEANT, THEY CALL HIM WRECK-IT RALPH FOR A REASON. HIS JOB IS TO WRECK THE NICELAND APARTMENT BUILDING SO FELIX CAN FIX IT WITH HIS MAGIC HAMMER AND GET HIS MEDAL.
OBSERVE WHILE I DEMONSTRATE ON THE MODEL, THEN IT'S YOUR TURN.
THIS OUGHTTA BE GOOD.
I'M GONNA WRECK IT!

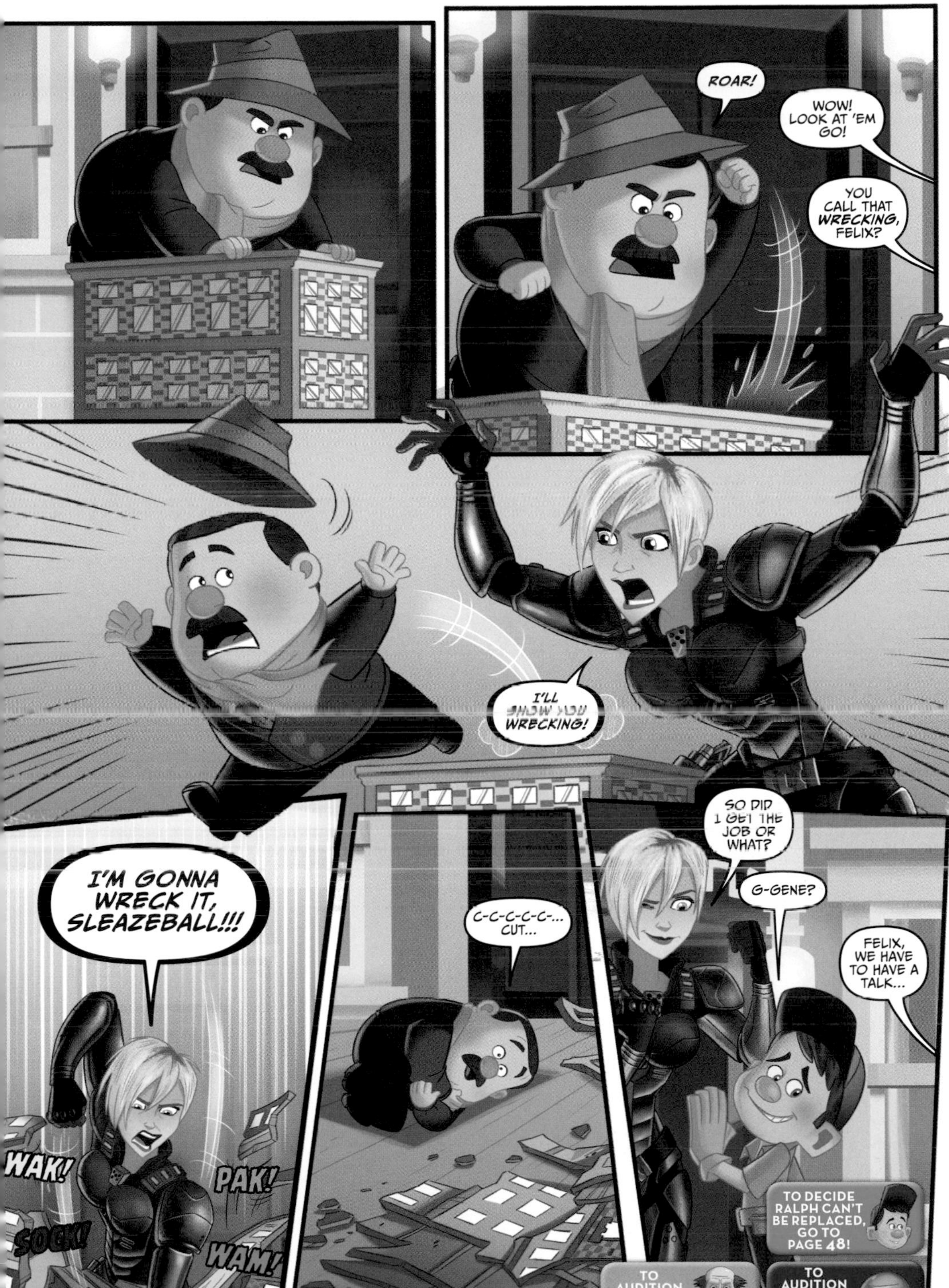
ROAR!
WOW! LOOK AT 'EM GO!
YOU CALL THAT WRECKING, FELIX?
I'LL
WRECKING!
I'M GONNA WRECK IT, SLEAZEBALL!!!
WAK!
PAK!
SOCK!
WAM!
C-C-C-C-C-... CUT...
SO DID I GET THE JOB OR WHAT?
G-GENE?
FELIX, WE HAVE TO HAVE A TALK...
TO DECIDE RALPH CAN'T BE REPLACED, GO TO PAGE 48!
TO AUDITION ZOMBIE, GO TO PAGE 24!
TO AUDITION SOUR BILL, GO TO PAGE 30!

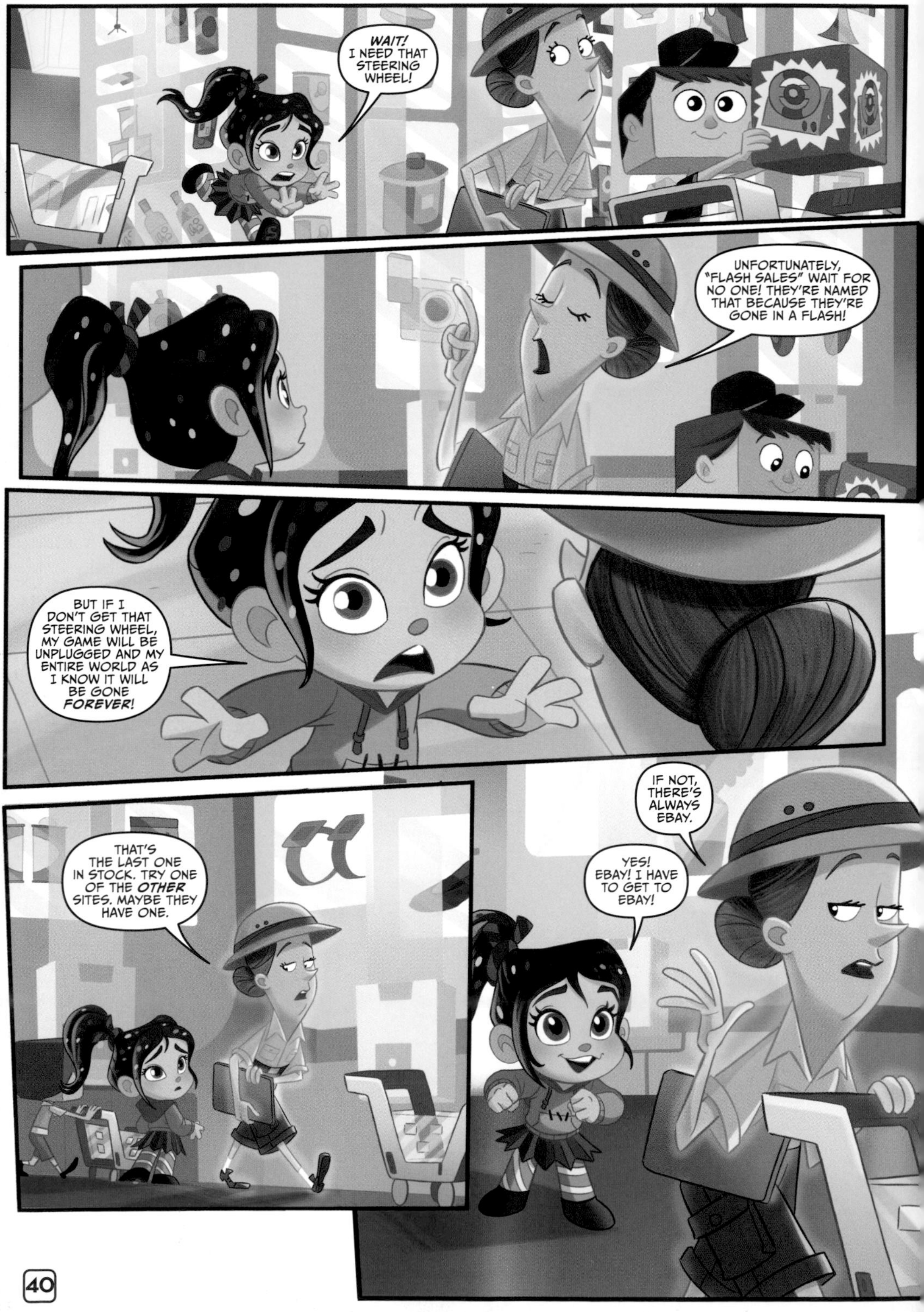
WAIT! I NEED THAT STEERING WHEEL!
UNFORTUNATELY, "FLASH SALES" WAIT FOR NO ONE! THEY'RE NAMED THAT BECAUSE THEY'RE GONE IN A FLASH!
BUT IF I DON'T GET THAT STEERING WHEEL, MY GAME WILL BE UNPLUGGED AND MY ENTIRE WORLD AS I KNOW IT WILL BE GONE FOREVER!
THAT'S THE LAST ONE IN STOCK. TRY ONE OF THE OTHER SITES. MAYBE THEY HAVE ONE.
IF NOT, THERE'S ALWAYS EBAY.
YES! EBAY! I HAVE TO GET TO EBAY!

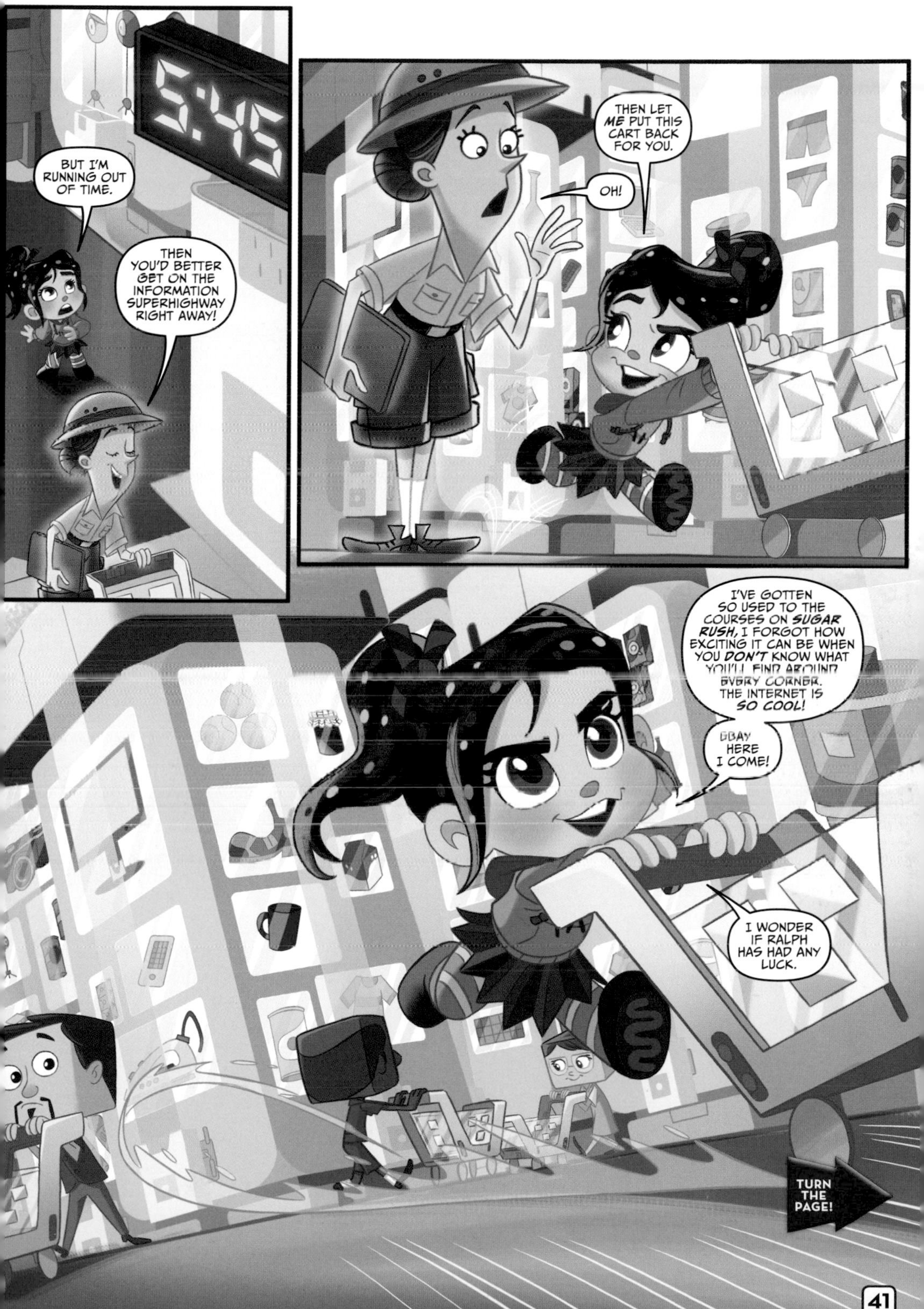
BUT I'M RUNNING OUT OF TIME.
THEN YOU'D BETTER GET ON THE INFORMATION SUPERHIGHWAY RIGHT AWAY!
THEN LET *ME* PUT THIS CART BACK FOR YOU.
OH!
I'VE GOTTEN SO USED TO THE COURSES ON *SUGAR RUSH*, I FORGOT HOW EXCITING IT CAN BE WHEN YOU *DON'T* KNOW WHAT YOU'LL FIND AROUND EVERY CORNER. THE INTERNET IS *SO COOL!*
EBAY HERE I COME!
I WONDER IF RALPH HAS HAD ANY LUCK.
TURN THE PAGE!

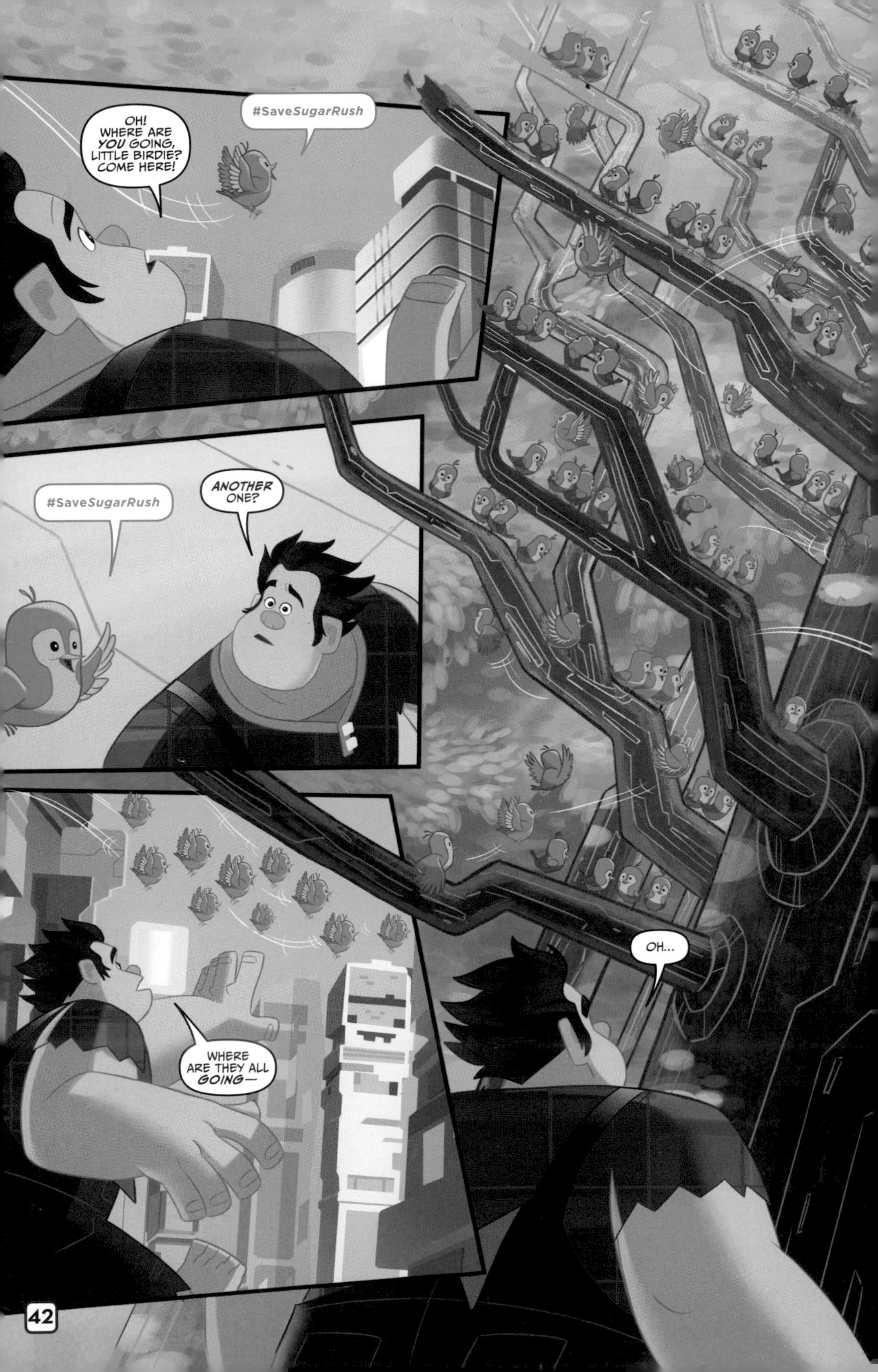
OH! WHERE ARE YOU GOING, LITTLE BIRDIE? COME HERE!
#SaveSugarRush
#SaveSugarRush
ANOTHER ONE?
WHERE ARE THEY ALL GOING—
OH...

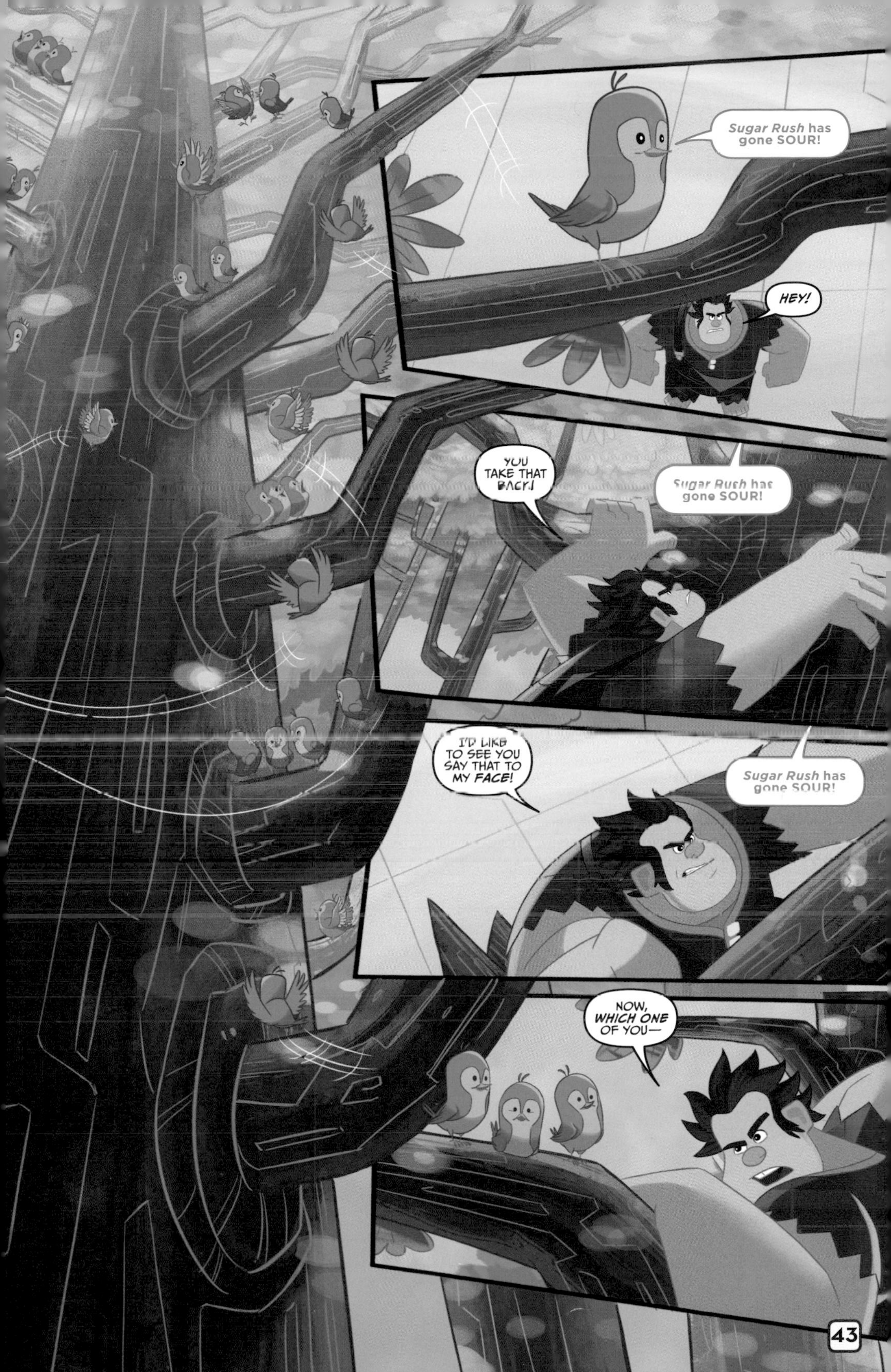

Sugar Rush has gone SOUR!
HEY!
YOU TAKE THAT BACK!
Sugar Rush has gone SOUR!
I'D LIKE TO SEE YOU SAY THAT TO MY *FACE!*
Sugar Rush has gone SOUR!
NOW, *WHICH ONE* OF YOU—

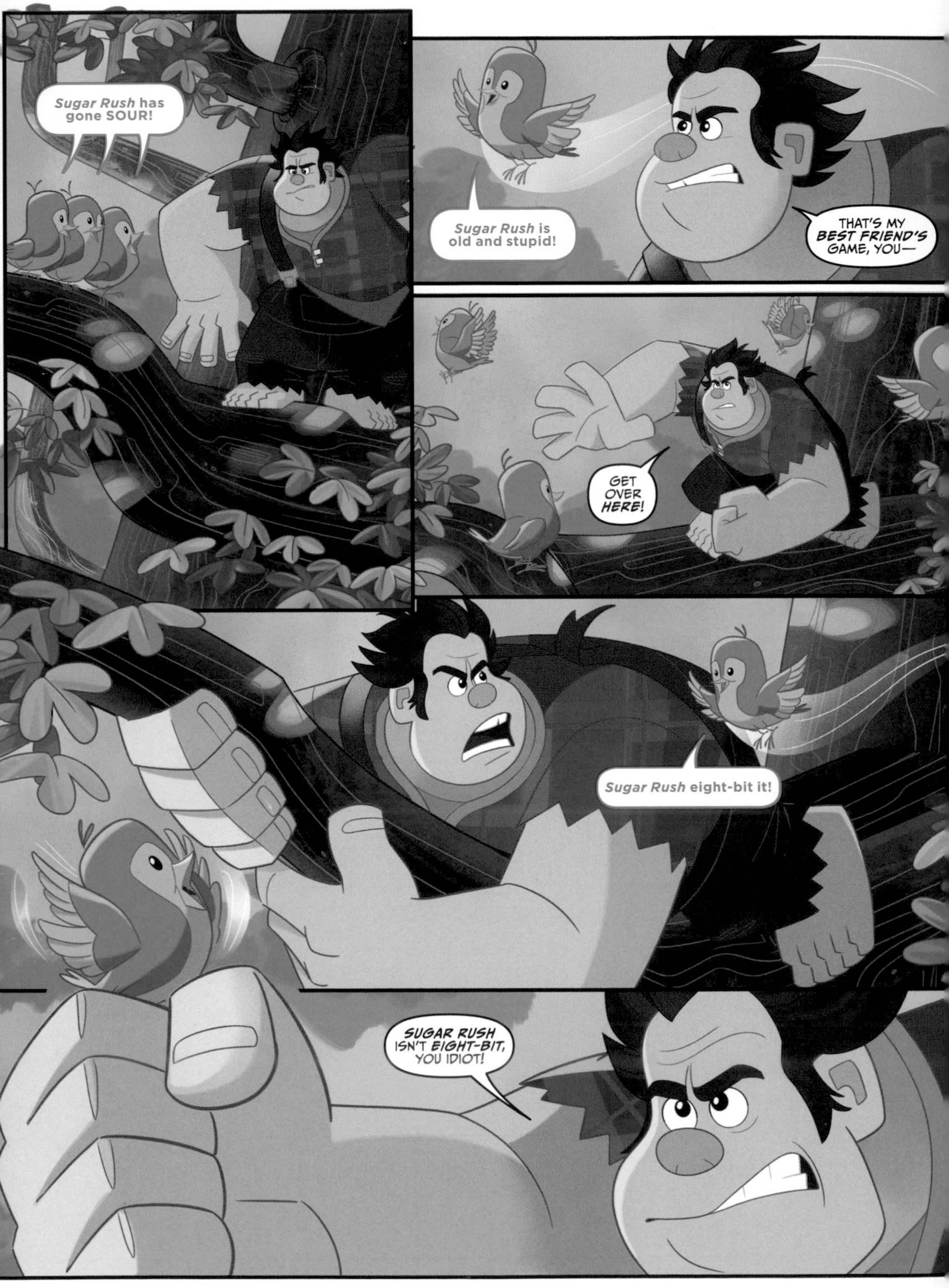
Sugar Rush has gone SOUR!
Sugar Rush is old and stupid!
THAT'S MY *BEST FRIEND'S* GAME, YOU—
GET OVER *HERE!*
Sugar Rush eight-bit it!
SUGAR RUSH ISN'T *EIGHT-BIT*, YOU IDIOT!

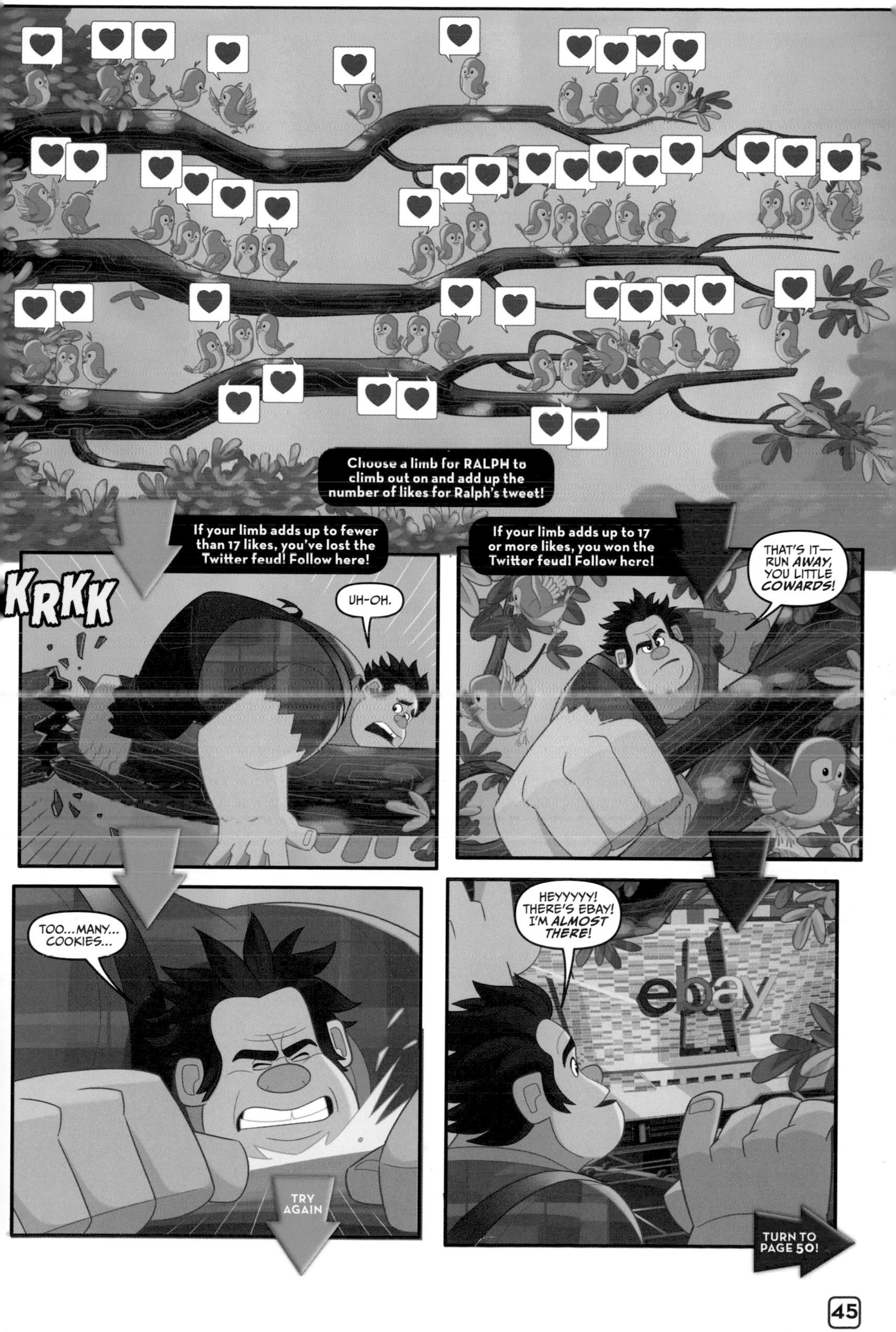
Choose a limb for RALPH to climb out on and add up the number of likes for Ralph's tweet!
If your limb adds up to fewer than 17 likes, you've lost the Twitter feud! Follow here!
If your limb adds up to 17 or more likes, you won the Twitter feud! Follow here!
KRKK
UH-OH.
THAT'S IT— RUN AWAY, YOU LITTLE COWARDS!
TOO...MANY... COOKIES...
HEYYYYY! THERE'S EBAY! I'M ALMOST THERE!
ebay
TRY AGAIN
TURN TO PAGE 50!

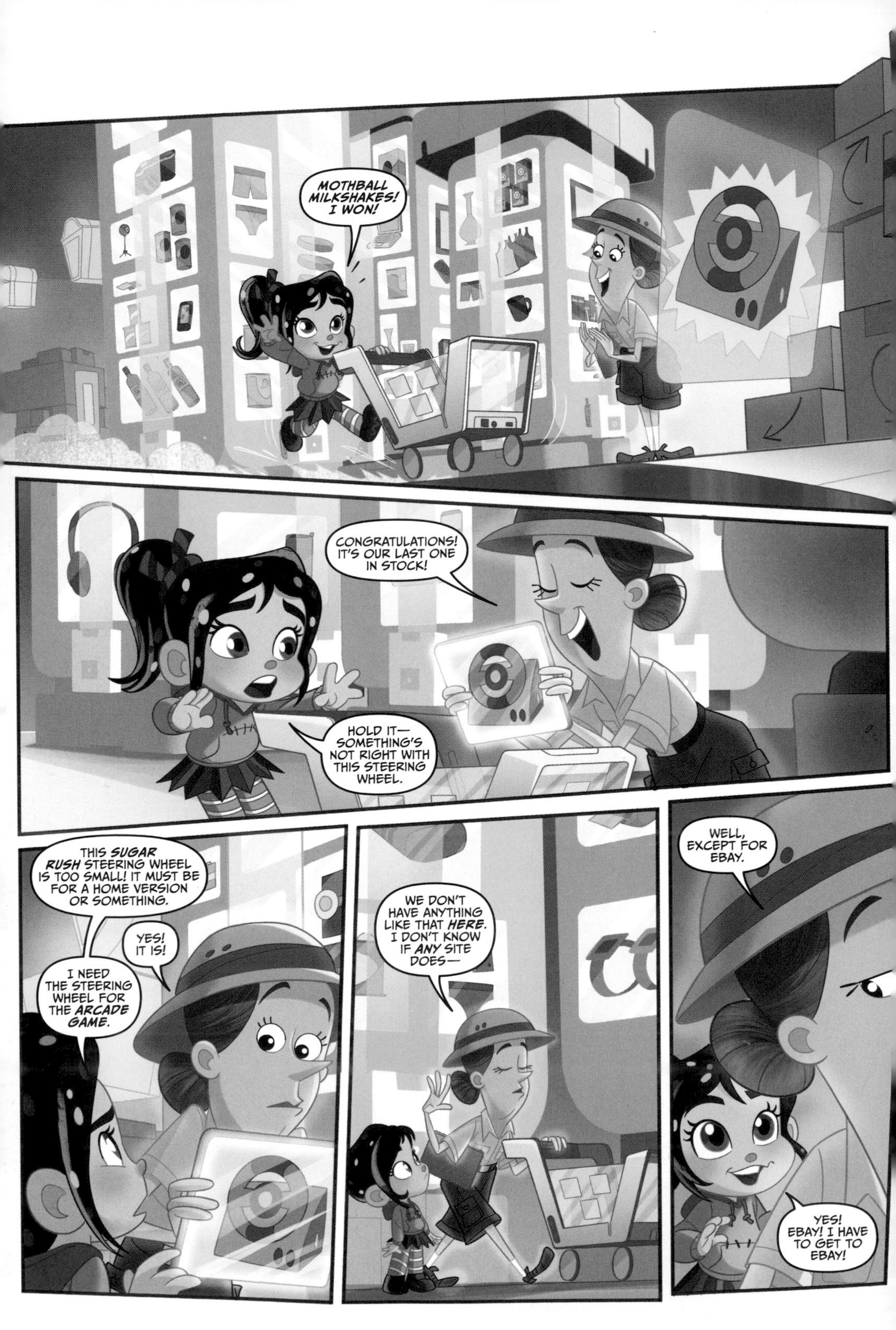
MOTHBALL MILKSHAKES! I WON!
CONGRATULATIONS! IT'S OUR LAST ONE IN STOCK!
HOLD IT— SOMETHING'S NOT RIGHT WITH THIS STEERING WHEEL.
THIS SUGAR RUSH STEERING WHEEL IS TOO SMALL! IT MUST BE FOR A HOME VERSION OR SOMETHING.
YES! IT IS!
I NEED THE STEERING WHEEL FOR THE ARCADE GAME.
WE DON'T HAVE ANYTHING LIKE THAT HERE. I DON'T KNOW IF ANY SITE DOES—
WELL, EXCEPT FOR EBAY.
YES! EBAY! I HAVE TO GET TO EBAY!

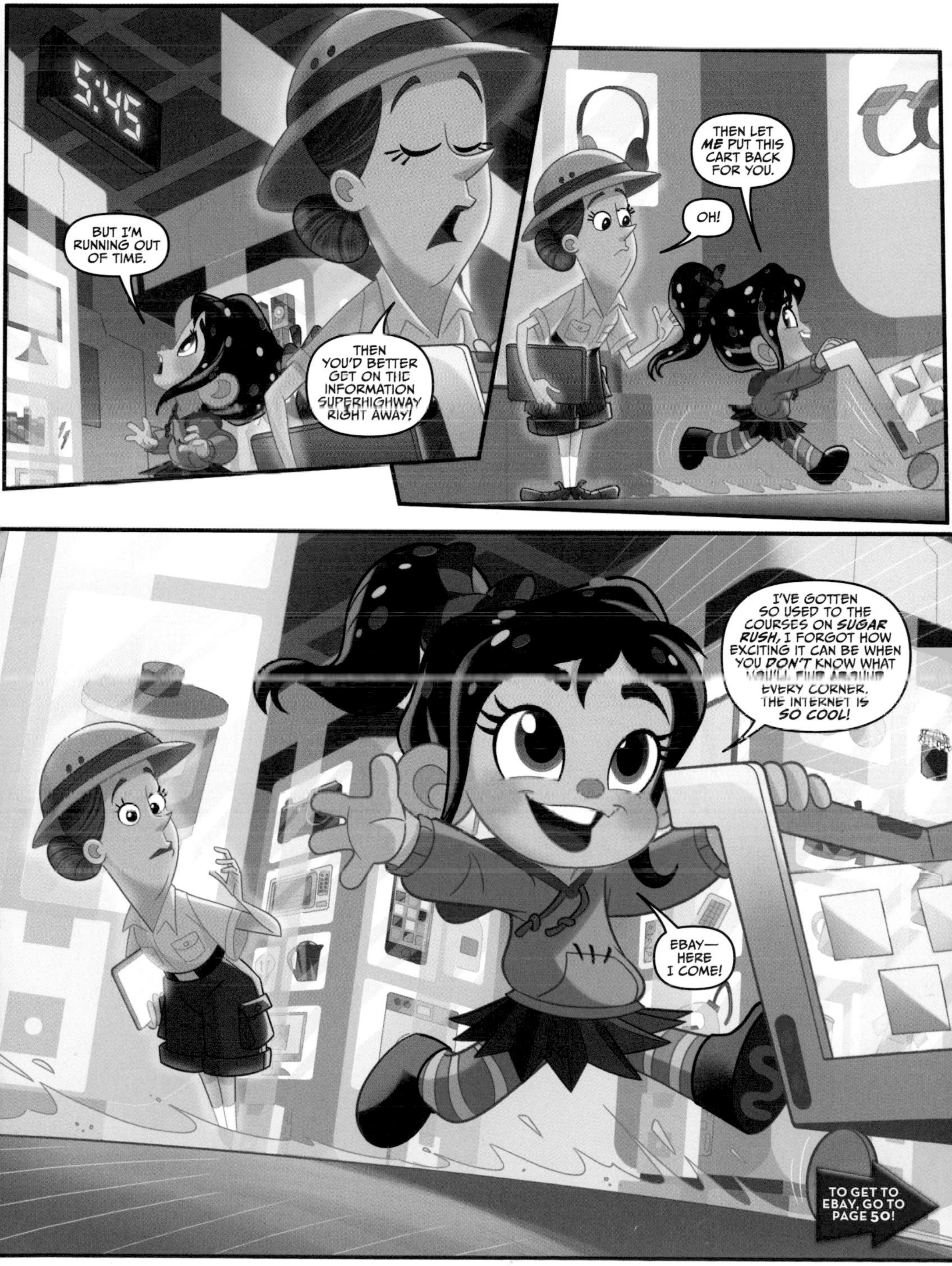
5:45
BUT I'M RUNNING OUT OF TIME.
THEN YOU'D BETTER GET ON THE INFORMATION SUPERHIGHWAY RIGHT AWAY!
THEN LET *ME* PUT THIS CART BACK FOR YOU.
OH!
I'VE GOTTEN SO USED TO THE COURSES ON *SUGAR RUSH*, I FORGOT HOW EXCITING IT CAN BE WHEN YOU *DON'T* KNOW WHAT
EVERY CORNER. THE INTERNET IS *SO COOL!*
EBAY— HERE I COME!
TO GET TO EBAY, GO TO PAGE 50!

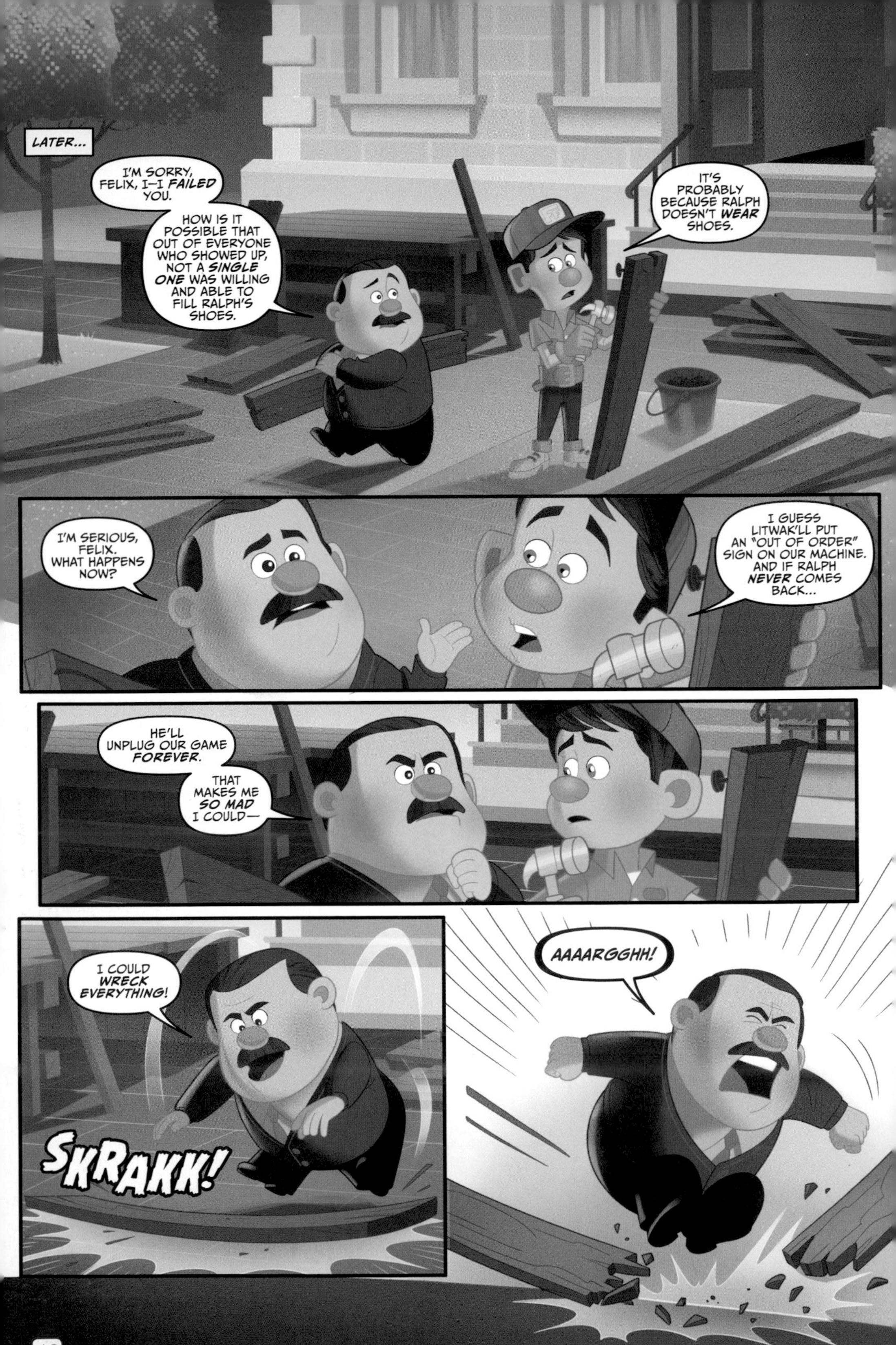
LATER...
I'M SORRY, FELIX, I—I FAILED YOU.
HOW IS IT POSSIBLE THAT OUT OF EVERYONE WHO SHOWED UP, NOT A SINGLE ONE WAS WILLING AND ABLE TO FILL RALPH'S SHOES.
IT'S PROBABLY BECAUSE RALPH DOESN'T WEAR SHOES.
I'M SERIOUS, FELIX. WHAT HAPPENS NOW?
I GUESS LITWAK'LL PUT AN "OUT OF ORDER" SIGN ON OUR MACHINE. AND IF RALPH NEVER COMES BACK...
HE'LL UNPLUG OUR GAME FOREVER.
THAT MAKES ME SO MAD I COULD—
I COULD WRECK EVERYTHING!
SKRAKK!
AAAARGGHH!

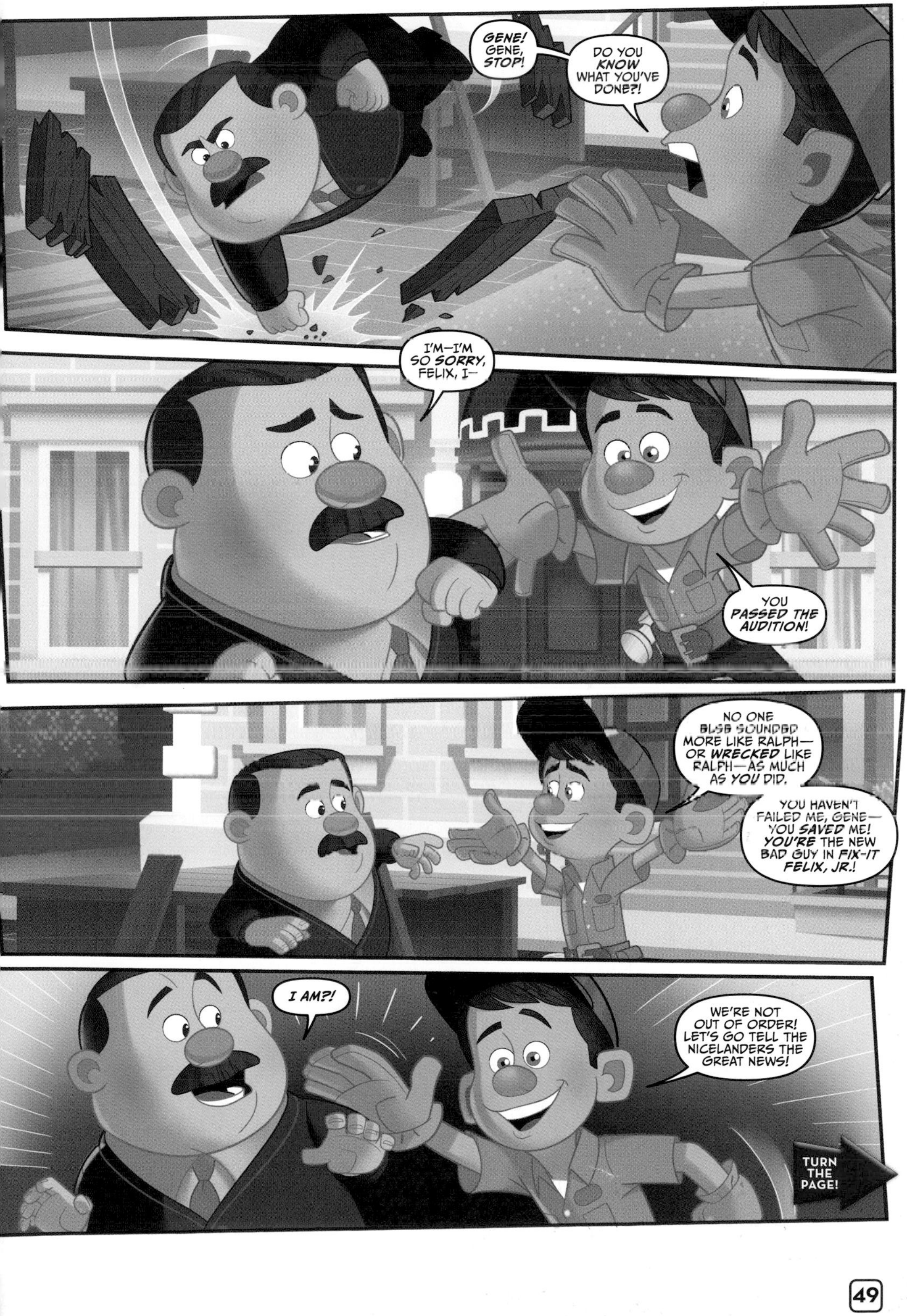
GENE! GENE, STOP!
DO YOU KNOW WHAT YOU'VE DONE?!
I'M—I'M SO SORRY, FELIX, I—
YOU PASSED THE AUDITION!
NO ONE ELSE SOUNDED MORE LIKE RALPH— OR WRECKED LIKE RALPH—AS MUCH AS YOU DID.
YOU HAVEN'T FAILED ME, GENE— YOU SAVED ME! YOU'RE THE NEW BAD GUY IN FIX-IT FELIX, JR.!
I AM?!
WE'RE NOT OUT OF ORDER! LET'S GO TELL THE NICELANDERS THE GREAT NEWS!
TURN THE PAGE!

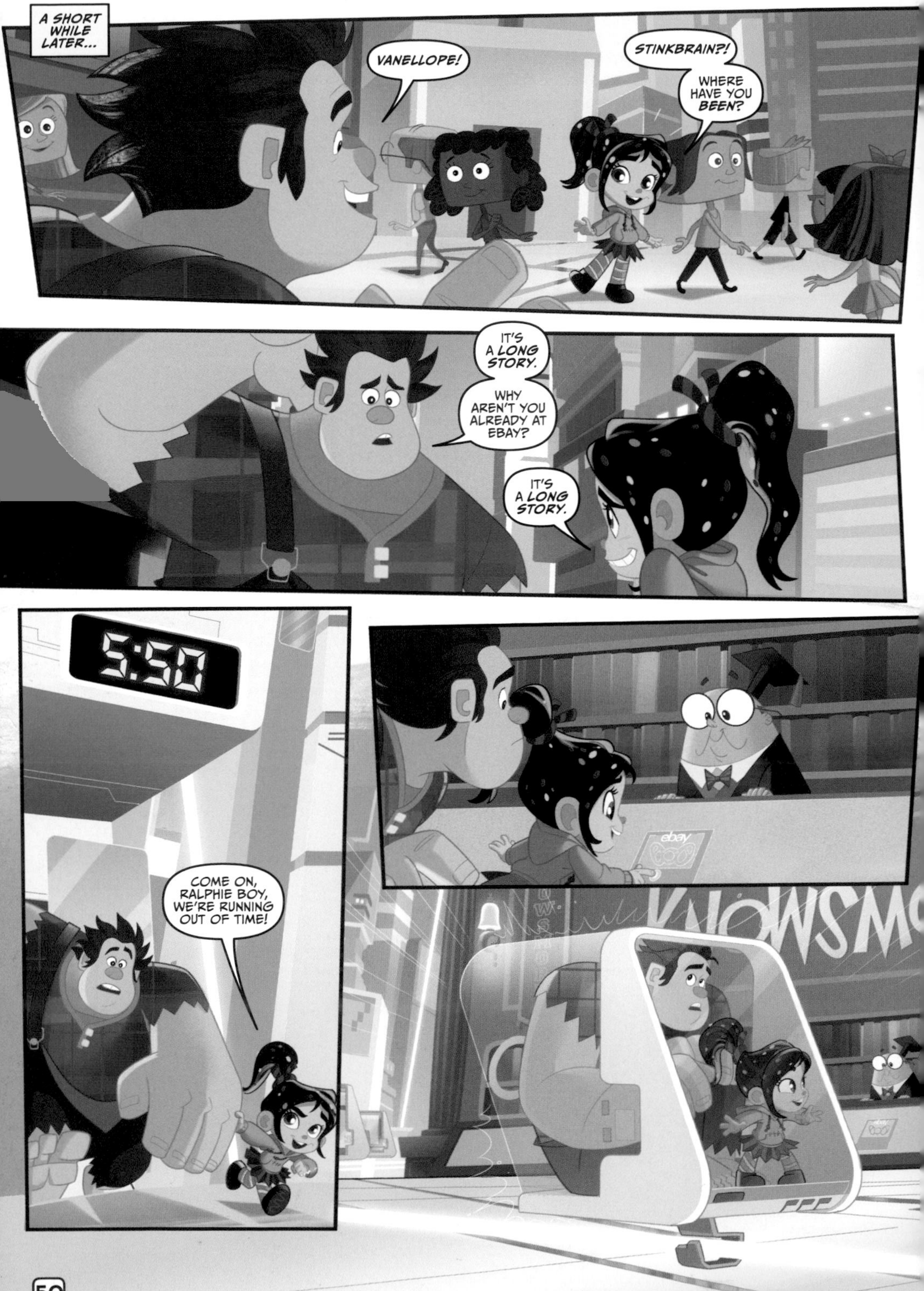
A SHORT WHILE LATER...
VANELLOPE!
STINKBRAIN?!
WHERE HAVE YOU BEEN?
IT'S A LONG STORY.
WHY AREN'T YOU ALREADY AT EBAY?
IT'S A LONG STORY.
5:50
ebay
COME ON, RALPHIE BOY, WE'RE RUNNING OUT OF TIME!
KNOWSMO

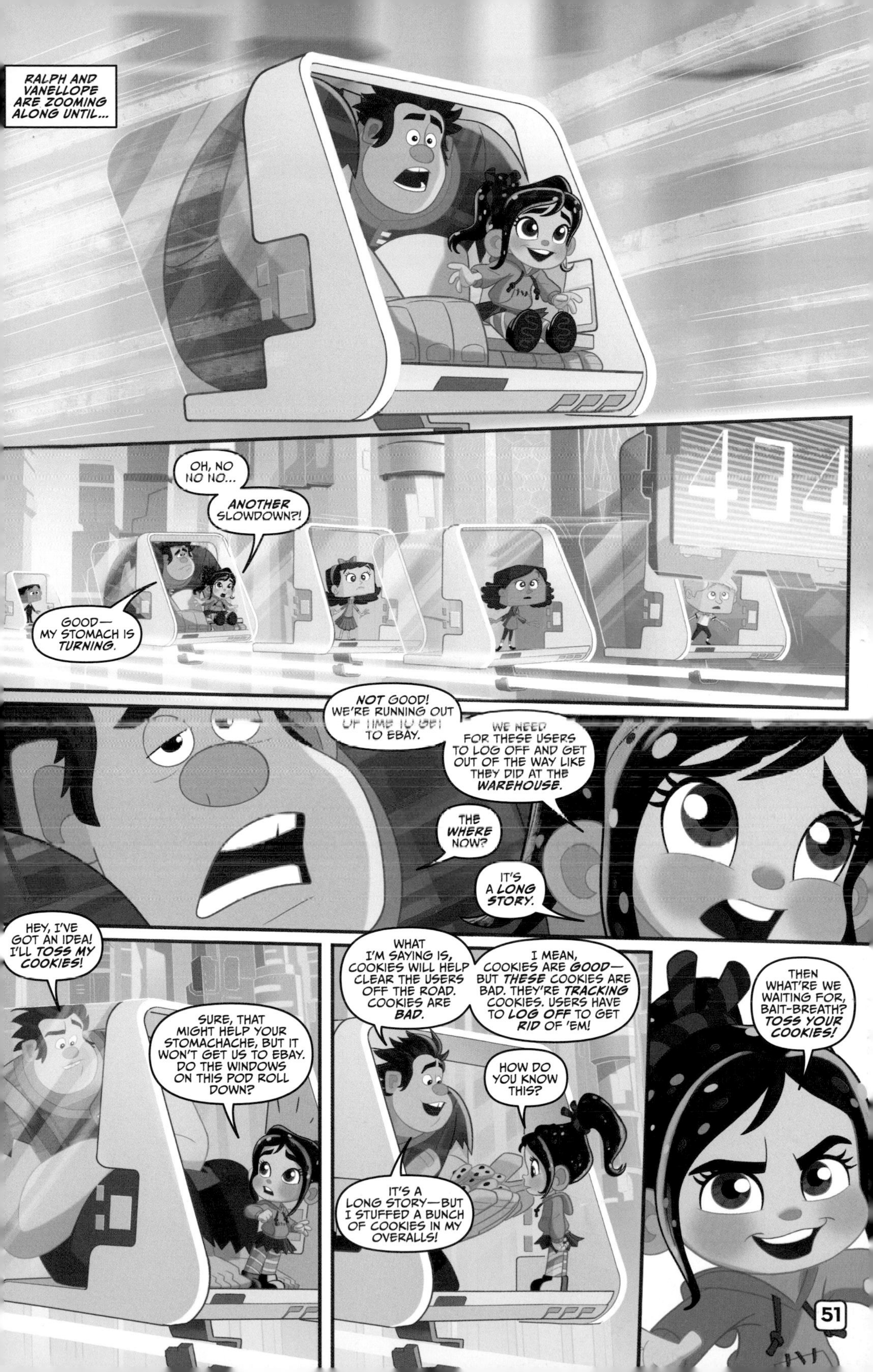
RALPH AND VANELLOPE ARE ZOOMING ALONG UNTIL...
OH, NO NO NO...
ANOTHER SLOWDOWN?!
GOOD— MY STOMACH IS TURNING.
404
NOT GOOD! WE'RE RUNNING OUT OF TIME TO GET TO EBAY.
WE NEED FOR THESE USERS TO LOG OFF AND GET OUT OF THE WAY LIKE THEY DID AT THE WAREHOUSE.
THE WHERE NOW?
IT'S A LONG STORY.
HEY, I'VE GOT AN IDEA! I'LL TOSS MY COOKIES!
SURE, THAT MIGHT HELP YOUR STOMACHACHE, BUT IT WON'T GET US TO EBAY. DO THE WINDOWS ON THIS POD ROLL DOWN?
WHAT I'M SAYING IS, COOKIES WILL HELP CLEAR THE USERS OFF THE ROAD. COOKIES ARE BAD.
I MEAN, COOKIES ARE GOOD— BUT THESE COOKIES ARE BAD. THEY'RE TRACKING COOKIES. USERS HAVE TO LOG OFF TO GET RID OF 'EM!
HOW DO YOU KNOW THIS?
IT'S A LONG STORY—BUT I STUFFED A BUNCH OF COOKIES IN MY OVERALLS!
THEN WHAT'RE WE WAITING FOR, BAIT-BREATH? TOSS YOUR COOKIES!

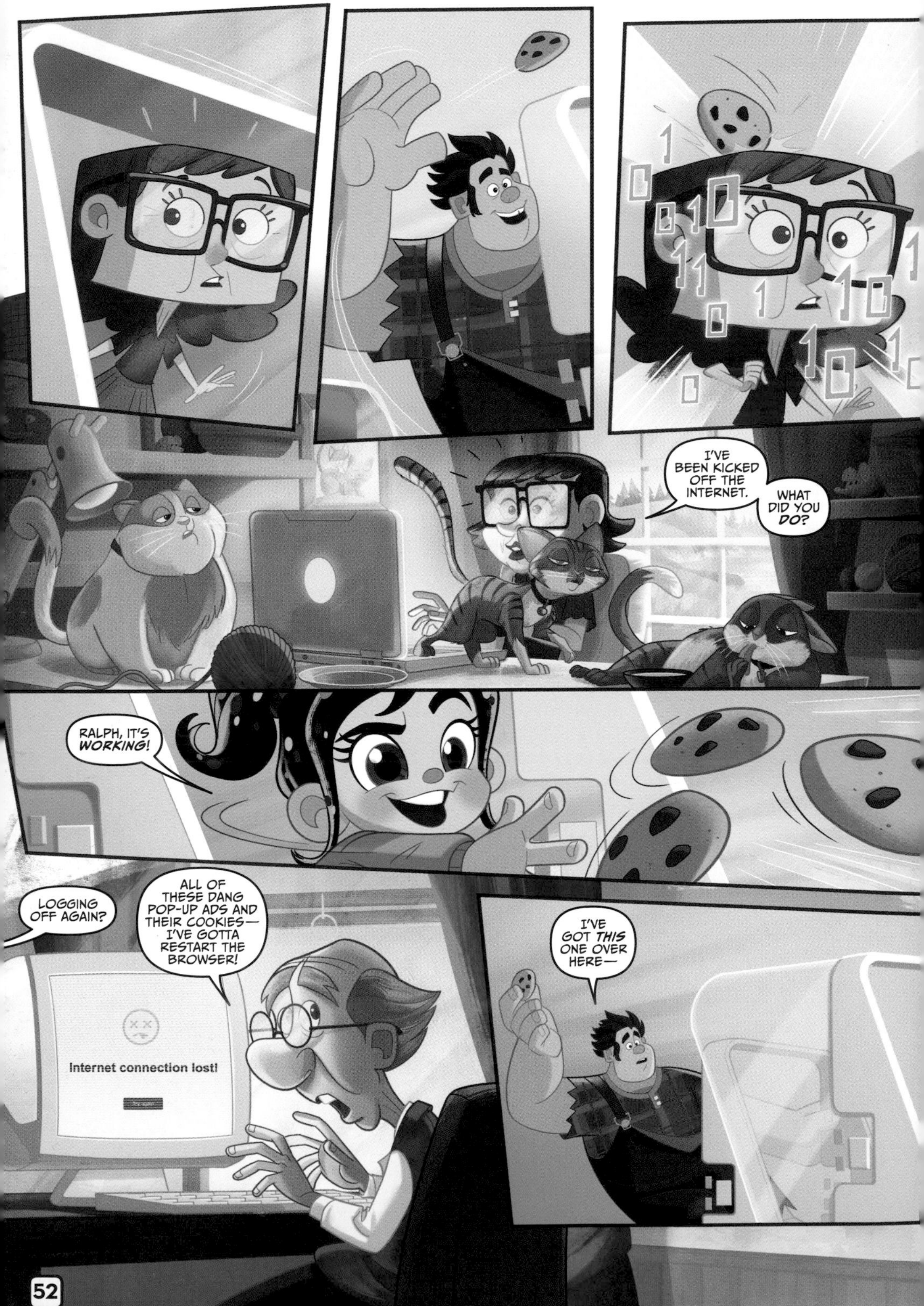
I'VE BEEN KICKED OFF THE INTERNET.
WHAT DID YOU *DO*?
RALPH, IT'S *WORKING*!
LOGGING OFF AGAIN?
ALL OF THESE DANG POP-UP ADS AND THEIR COOKIES— I'VE GOTTA RESTART THE BROWSER!
Internet connection lost!
I'VE GOT *THIS* ONE OVER HERE—

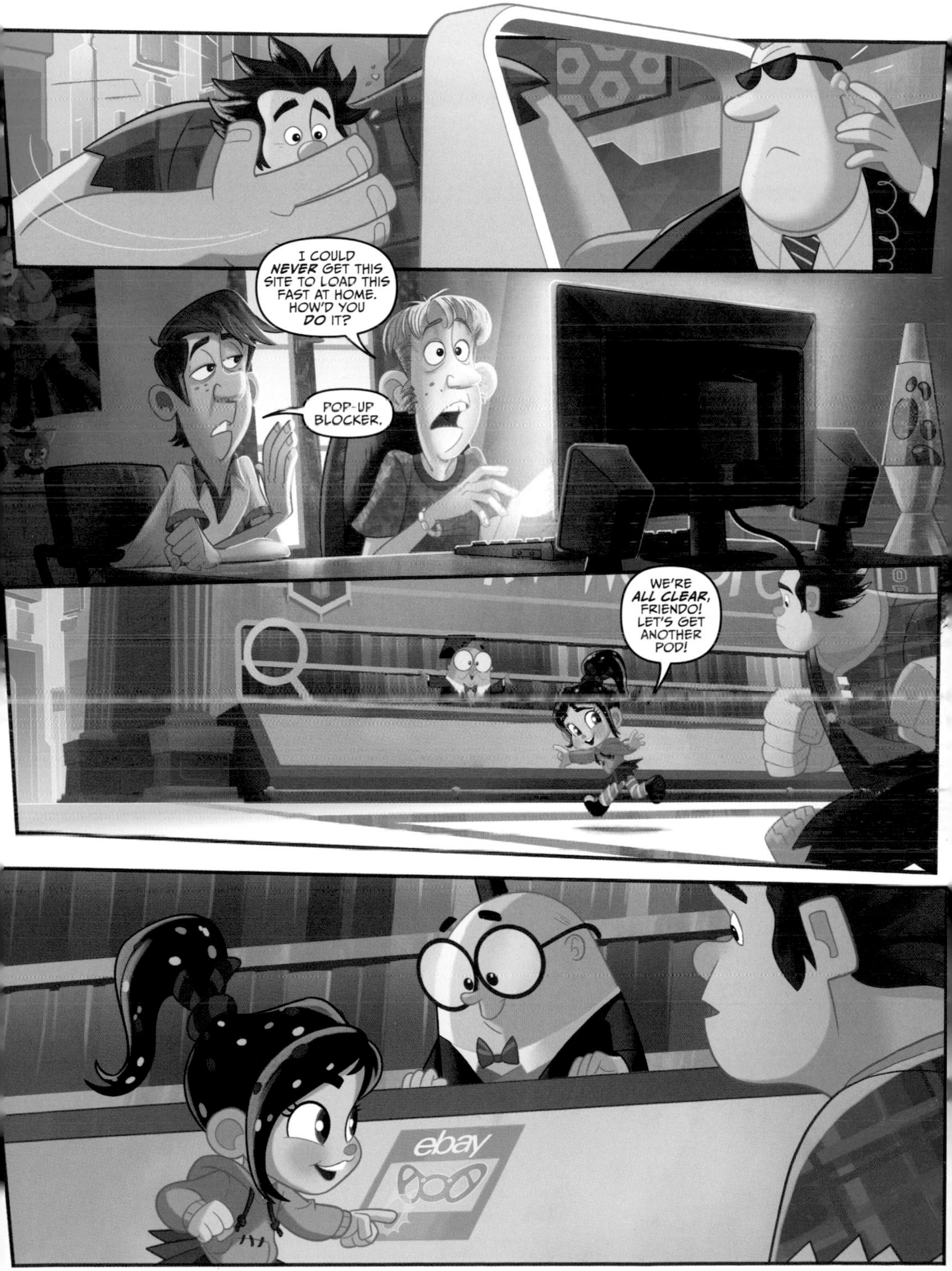
I COULD *NEVER* GET THIS SITE TO LOAD THIS FAST AT HOME. HOW'D YOU *DO* IT?
POP-UP BLOCKER.
WE'RE *ALL CLEAR*, FRIENDO! LET'S GET ANOTHER POD!
ebay

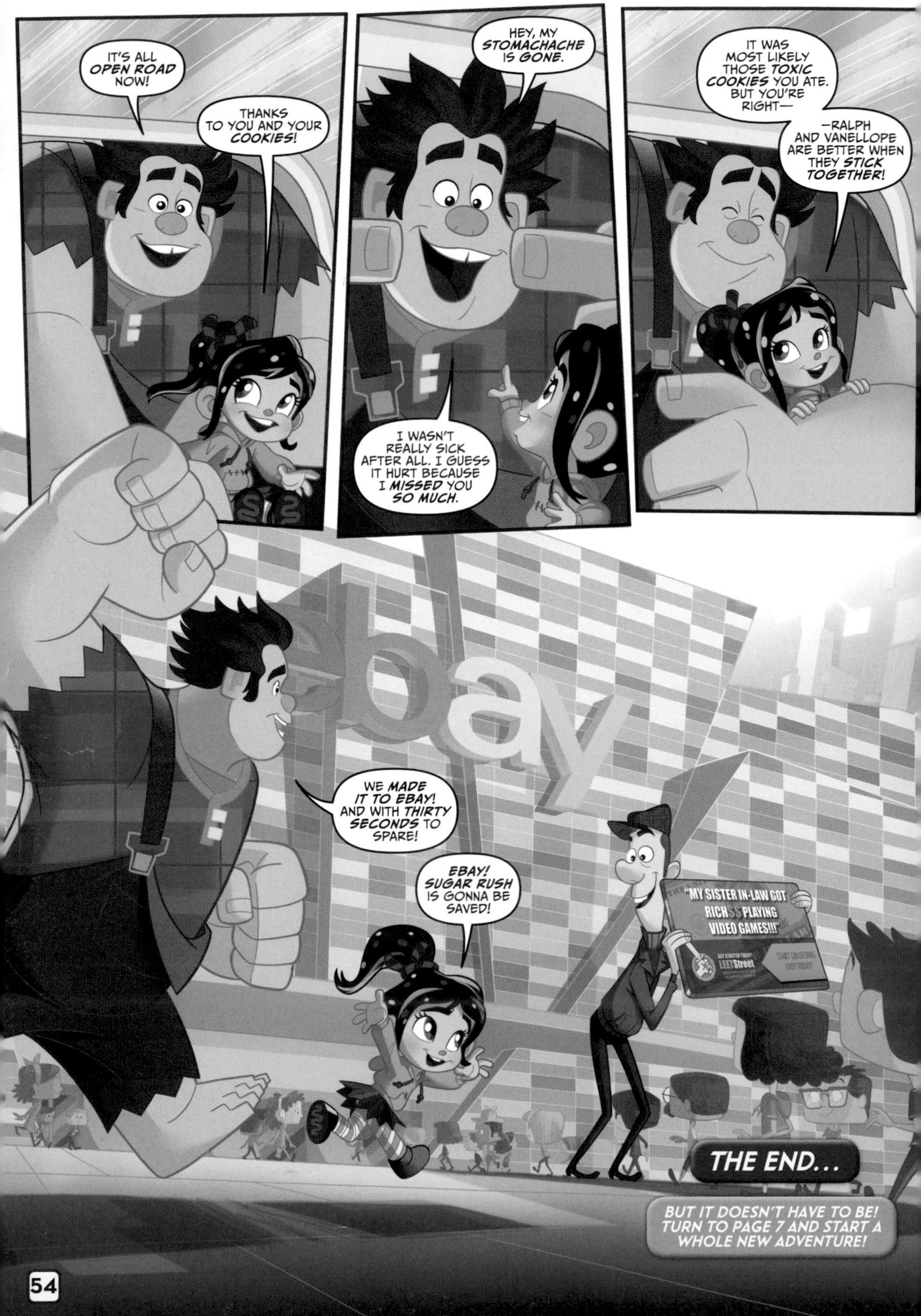
IT'S ALL OPEN ROAD NOW!
THANKS TO YOU AND YOUR COOKIES!
HEY, MY STOMACHACHE IS GONE.
I WASN'T REALLY SICK AFTER ALL. I GUESS IT HURT BECAUSE I MISSED YOU SO MUCH.
IT WAS MOST LIKELY THOSE TOXIC COOKIES YOU ATE. BUT YOU'RE RIGHT—
—RALPH AND VANELLOPE ARE BETTER WHEN THEY STICK TOGETHER!
ebay
WE MADE IT TO EBAY! AND WITH THIRTY SECONDS TO SPARE!
EBAY! SUGAR RUSH IS GONNA BE SAVED!
"MY SISTER IN-LAW GOT RICH$$ PLAYING VIDEO GAMES!!!"
LEETStreet
THE END...

BUT IT DOESN'T HAVE TO BE! TURN TO PAGE 7 AND START A WHOLE NEW ADVENTURE!

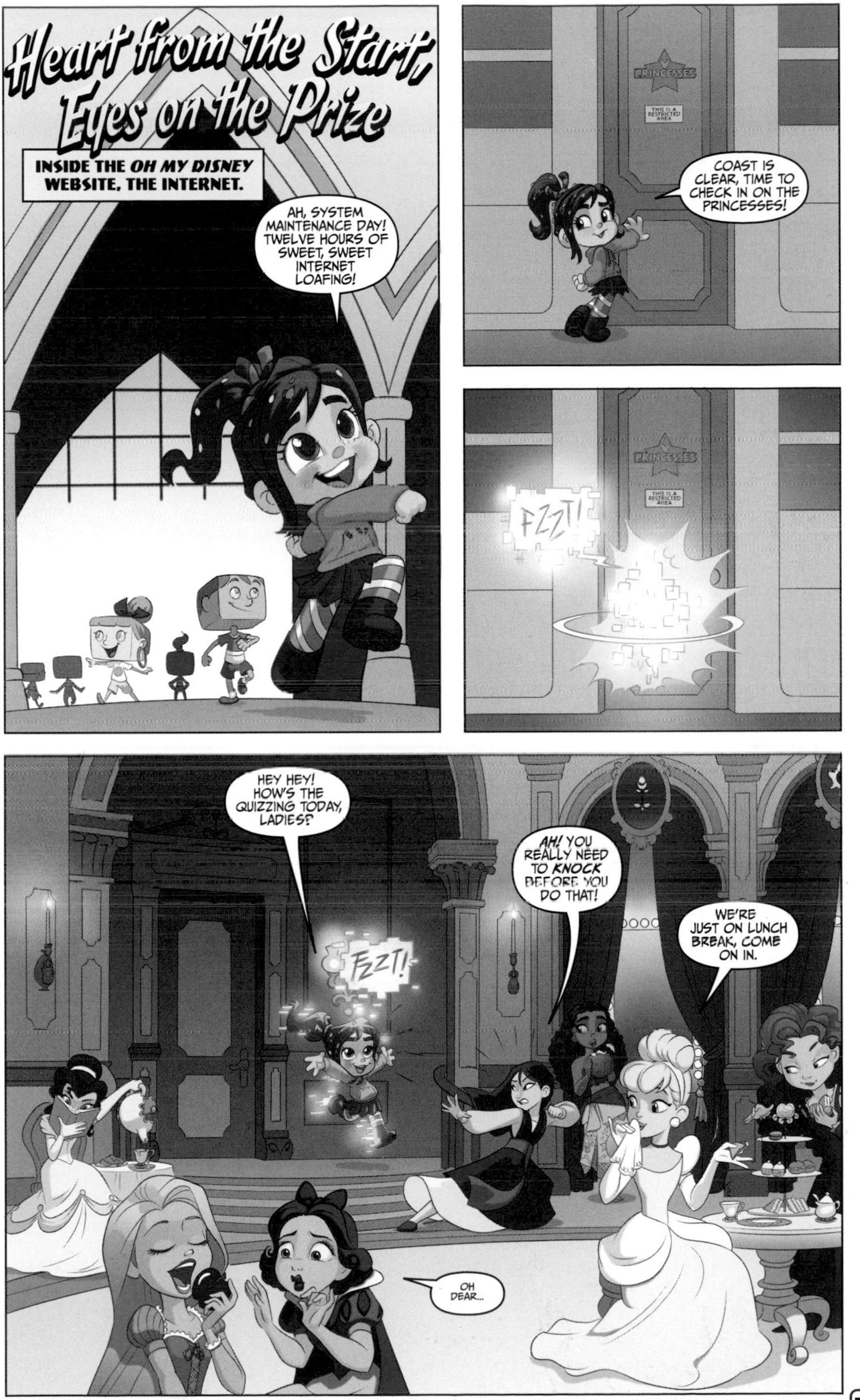
Heart from the Start, Eyes on the Prize
INSIDE THE *OH MY DISNEY* WEBSITE, THE INTERNET.
AH, SYSTEM MAINTENANCE DAY! TWELVE HOURS OF SWEET, SWEET INTERNET LOAFING!
PRINCESSES
THIS IS A RESTRICTED AREA
COAST IS CLEAR, TIME TO CHECK IN ON THE PRINCESSES!
PRINCESSES
THIS IS A RESTRICTED AREA
FZZT!
HEY HEY! HOW'S THE QUIZZING TODAY, LADIES?
FZZT!
AH! YOU REALLY NEED TO ***KNOCK*** BEFORE YOU DO THAT!
WE'RE JUST ON LUNCH BREAK, COME ON IN.
OH DEAR...

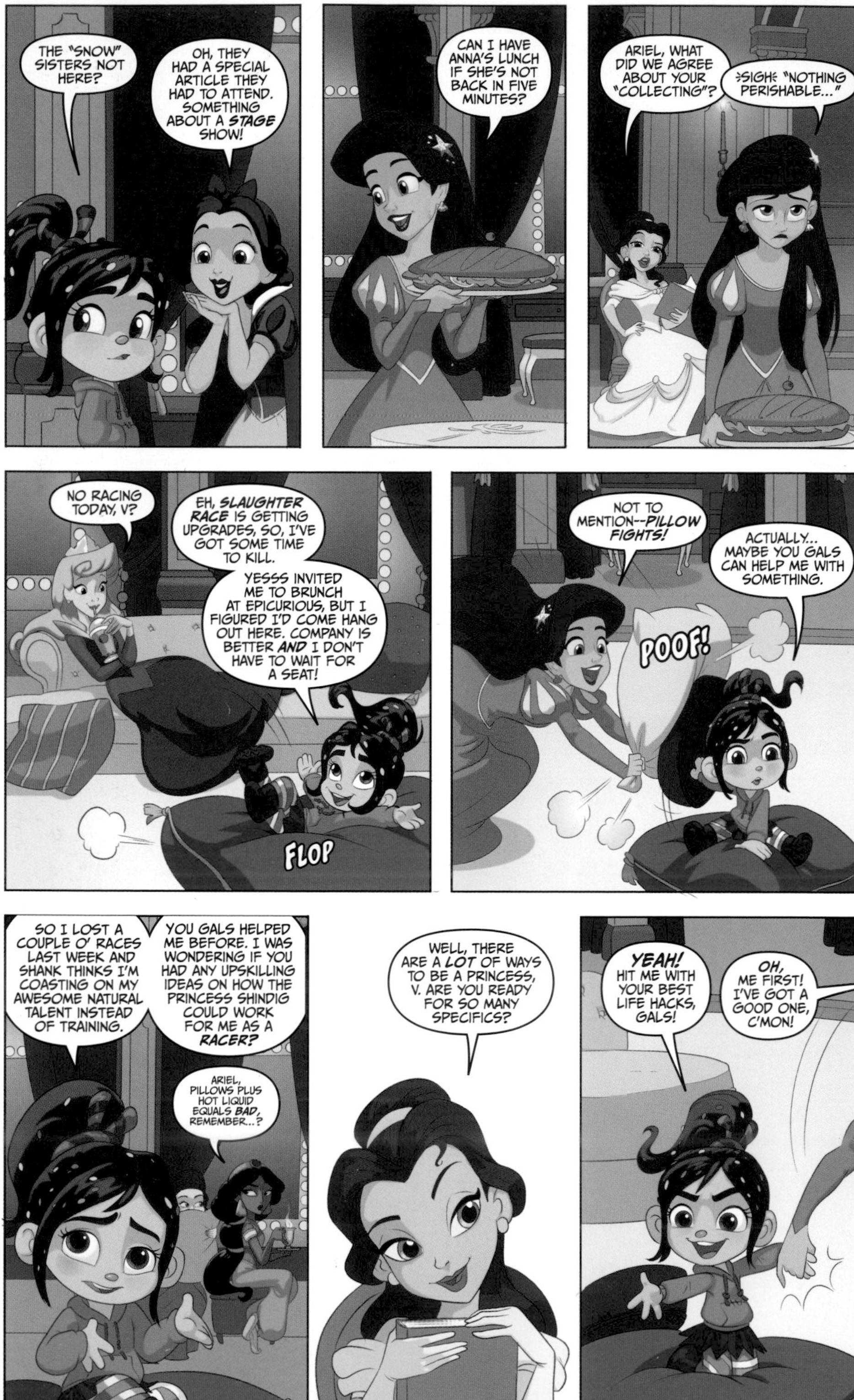
THE "SNOW" SISTERS NOT HERE?
OH, THEY HAD A SPECIAL ARTICLE THEY HAD TO ATTEND. SOMETHING ABOUT A STAGE SHOW!
CAN I HAVE ANNA'S LUNCH IF SHE'S NOT BACK IN FIVE MINUTES?
ARIEL, WHAT DID WE AGREE ABOUT YOUR "COLLECTING"?
SIGH "NOTHING PERISHABLE..."
NO RACING TODAY, V?
EH, SLAUGHTER RACE IS GETTING UPGRADES, SO, I'VE GOT SOME TIME TO KILL.
YESSS INVITED ME TO BRUNCH AT EPICURIOUS, BUT I FIGURED I'D COME HANG OUT HERE. COMPANY IS BETTER AND I DON'T HAVE TO WAIT FOR A SEAT!
FLOP
NOT TO MENTION--PILLOW FIGHTS!
POOF!
ACTUALLY... MAYBE YOU GALS CAN HELP ME WITH SOMETHING.
SO I LOST A COUPLE O' RACES LAST WEEK AND SHANK THINKS I'M COASTING ON MY AWESOME NATURAL TALENT INSTEAD OF TRAINING.
YOU GALS HELPED ME BEFORE. I WAS WONDERING IF YOU HAD ANY UPSKILLING IDEAS ON HOW THE PRINCESS SHINDIG COULD WORK FOR ME AS A RACER?
ARIEL, PILLOWS PLUS HOT LIQUID EQUALS BAD, REMEMBER...?
WELL, THERE ARE A LOT OF WAYS TO BE A PRINCESS, V. ARE YOU READY FOR SO MANY SPECIFICS?
YEAH! HIT ME WITH YOUR BEST LIFE HACKS, GALS!
OH, ME FIRST! I'VE GOT A GOOD ONE, C'MON!

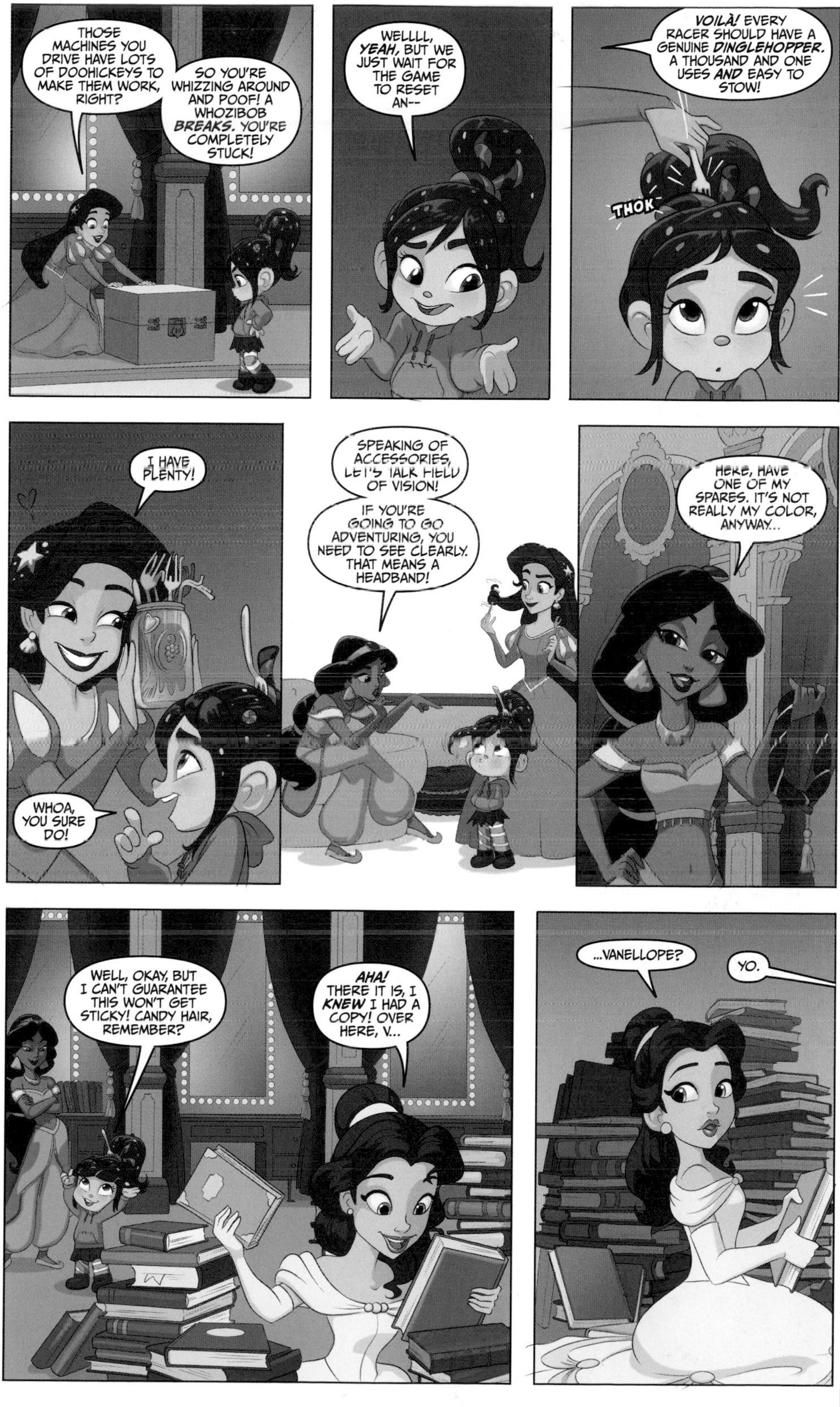
THOSE MACHINES YOU DRIVE HAVE LOTS OF DOOHICKEYS TO MAKE THEM WORK, RIGHT?
SO YOU'RE WHIZZING AROUND AND POOF! A WHOZIBOB BREAKS. YOU'RE COMPLETELY STUCK!
WELLLL, YEAH, BUT WE JUST WAIT FOR THE GAME TO RESET AN--
VOILÀ! EVERY RACER SHOULD HAVE A GENUINE DINGLEHOPPER. A THOUSAND AND ONE USES AND EASY TO STOW!
THOK
I HAVE PLENTY!
WHOA, YOU SURE DO!
SPEAKING OF ACCESSORIES, LET'S TALK FIELD OF VISION!
IF YOU'RE GOING TO GO ADVENTURING, YOU NEED TO SEE CLEARLY. THAT MEANS A HEADBAND!
HERE, HAVE ONE OF MY SPARES. IT'S NOT REALLY MY COLOR, ANYWAY...
WELL, OKAY, BUT I CAN'T GUARANTEE THIS WON'T GET STICKY! CANDY HAIR, REMEMBER?
AHA! THERE IT IS, I KNEW I HAD A COPY! OVER HERE, V...
...VANELLOPE?
YO.

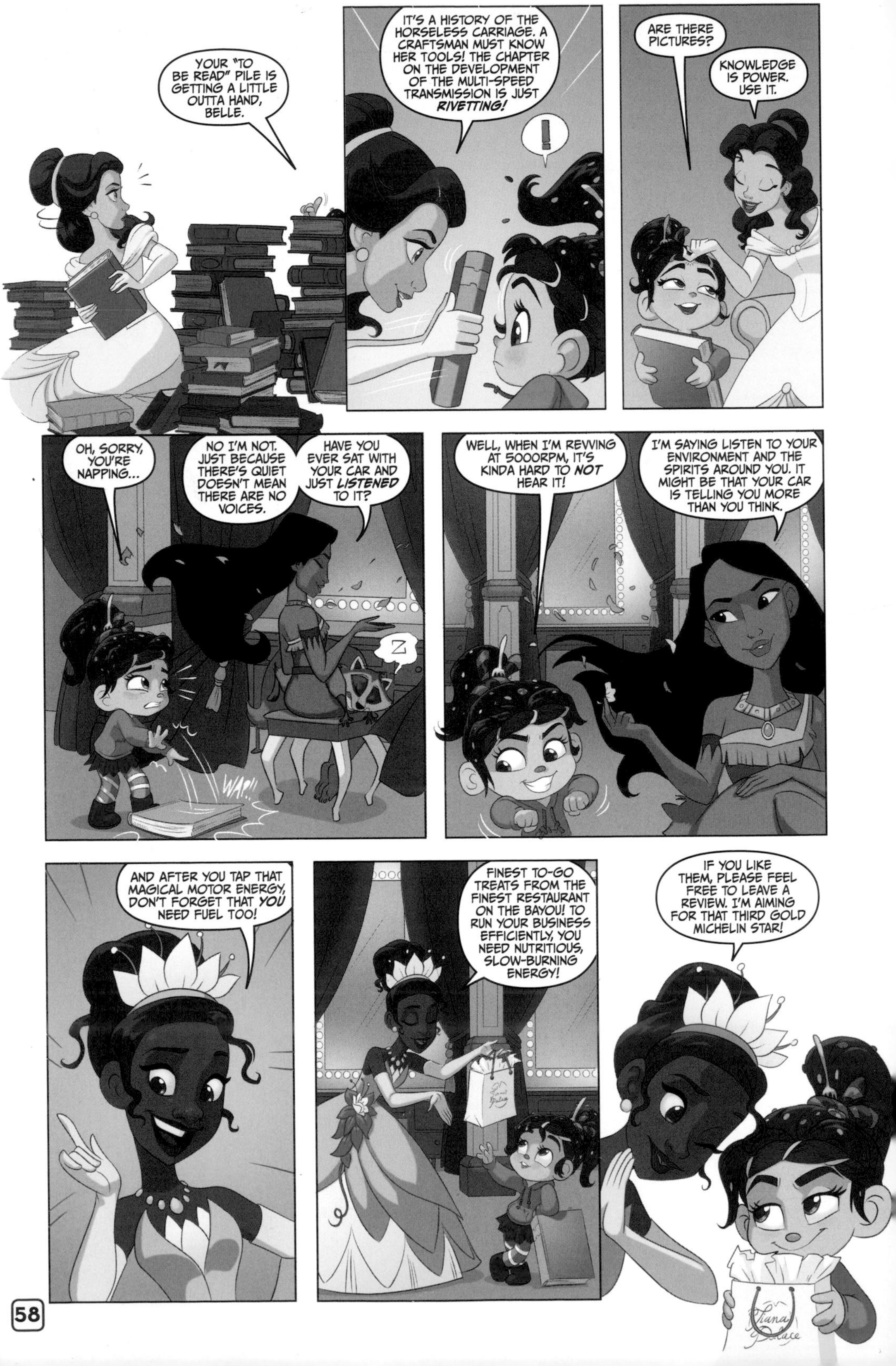

YOUR "TO BE READ" PILE IS GETTING A LITTLE OUTTA HAND, BELLE.
IT'S A HISTORY OF THE HORSELESS CARRIAGE. A CRAFTSMAN MUST KNOW HER TOOLS! THE CHAPTER ON THE DEVELOPMENT OF THE MULTI-SPEED TRANSMISSION IS JUST RIVETTING!
!
ARE THERE PICTURES?
KNOWLEDGE IS POWER. USE IT.
OH, SORRY, YOU'RE NAPPING...
NO I'M NOT. JUST BECAUSE THERE'S QUIET DOESN'T MEAN THERE ARE NO VOICES.
HAVE YOU EVER SAT WITH YOUR CAR AND JUST LISTENED TO IT?
Z
WAP!!
WELL, WHEN I'M REVVING AT 5000RPM, IT'S KINDA HARD TO NOT HEAR IT!
I'M SAYING LISTEN TO YOUR ENVIRONMENT AND THE SPIRITS AROUND YOU. IT MIGHT BE THAT YOUR CAR IS TELLING YOU MORE THAN YOU THINK.
AND AFTER YOU TAP THAT MAGICAL MOTOR ENERGY, DON'T FORGET THAT YOU NEED FUEL TOO!
FINEST TO-GO TREATS FROM THE FINEST RESTAURANT ON THE BAYOU! TO RUN YOUR BUSINESS EFFICIENTLY, YOU NEED NUTRITIOUS, SLOW-BURNING ENERGY!
IF YOU LIKE THEM, PLEASE FEEL FREE TO LEAVE A REVIEW. I'M AIMING FOR THAT THIRD GOLD MICHELIN STAR!

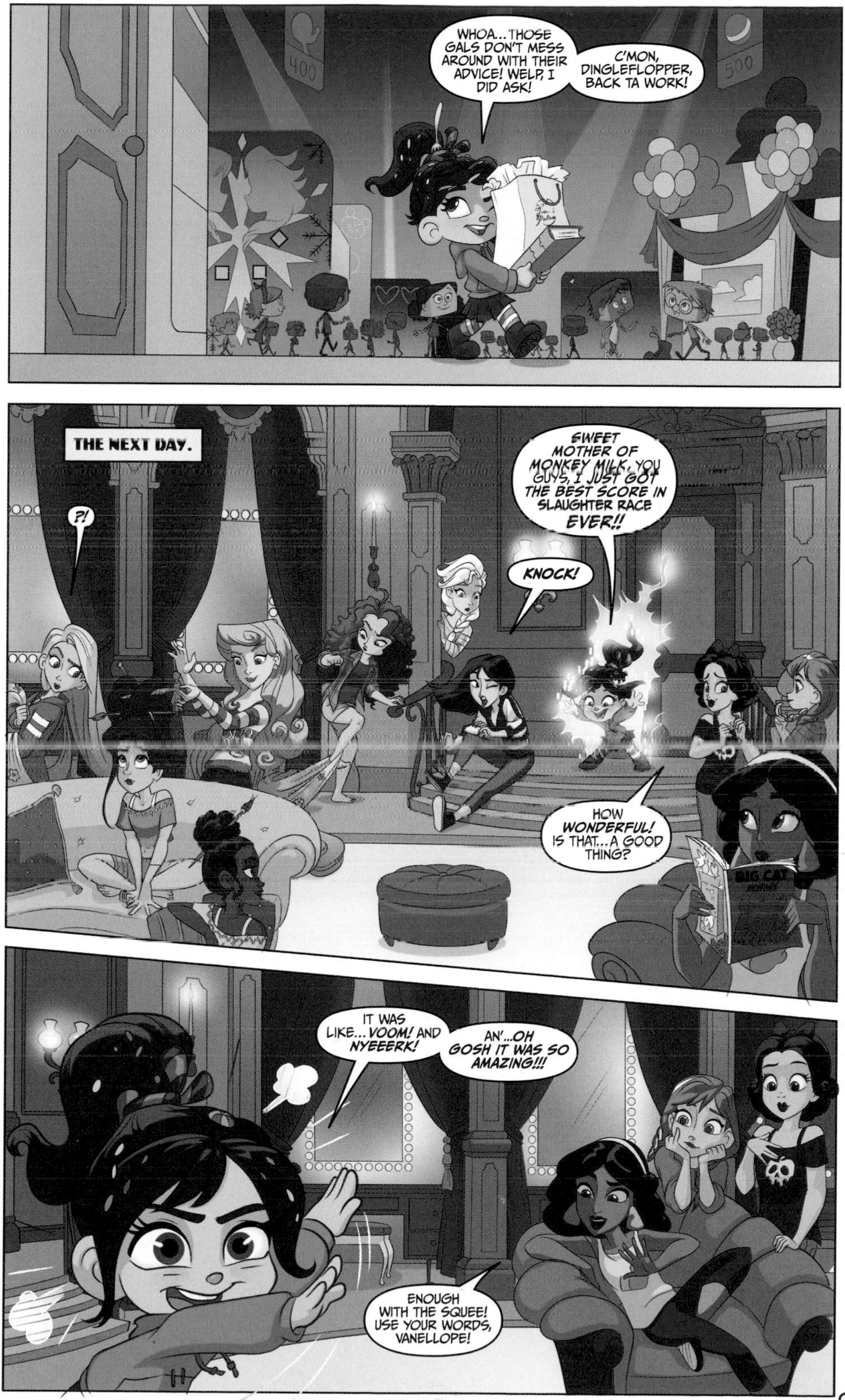

WHOA...THOSE GALS DON'T MESS AROUND WITH THEIR ADVICE! WELP, I DID ASK!
C'MON, DINGLEFLOPPER, BACK TA WORK!
THE NEXT DAY.
?!
SWEET MOTHER OF MONKEY MILK, YOU GUYS, I JUST GOT THE BEST SCORE IN SLAUGHTER RACE EVER!!
KNOCK!
HOW WONDERFUL! IS THAT...A GOOD THING?
BIG CAT
IT WAS LIKE...VOOM! AND NYEEERK!
AN'...OH GOSH IT WAS SO AMAZING!!!
ENOUGH WITH THE SQUEE! USE YOUR WORDS, VANELLOPE!

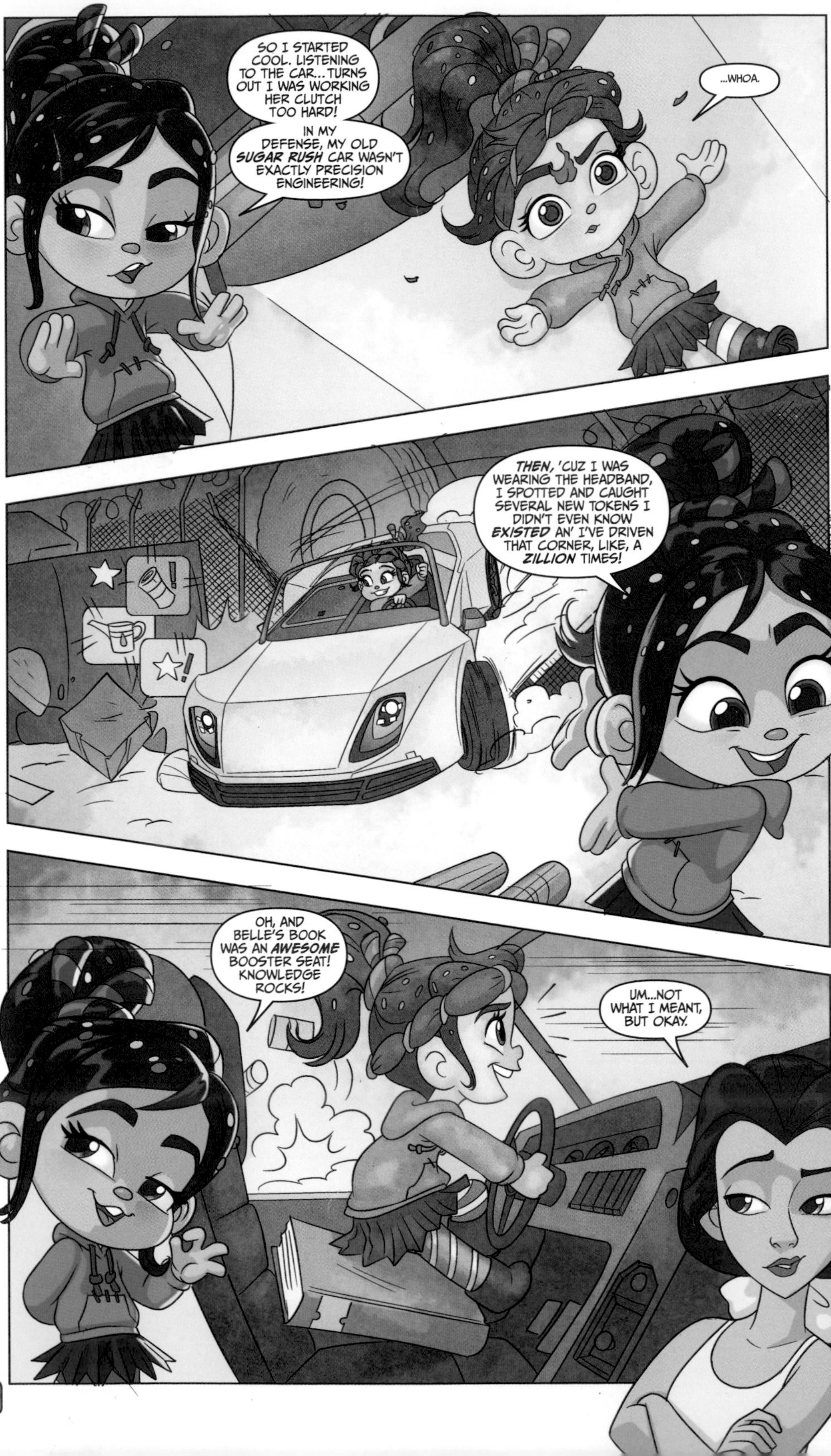
SO I STARTED COOL. LISTENING TO THE CAR...TURNS OUT I WAS WORKING HER CLUTCH TOO HARD!
IN MY DEFENSE, MY OLD *SUGAR RUSH* CAR WASN'T EXACTLY PRECISION ENGINEERING!
...WHOA.
THEN, 'CUZ I WAS WEARING THE HEADBAND, I SPOTTED AND CAUGHT SEVERAL NEW TOKENS I DIDN'T EVEN KNOW *EXISTED* AN' I'VE DRIVEN THAT CORNER, LIKE, A *ZILLION* TIMES!
OH, AND BELLE'S BOOK WAS AN *AWESOME* BOOSTER SEAT! KNOWLEDGE ROCKS!
UM...NOT WHAT I MEANT, BUT OKAY.

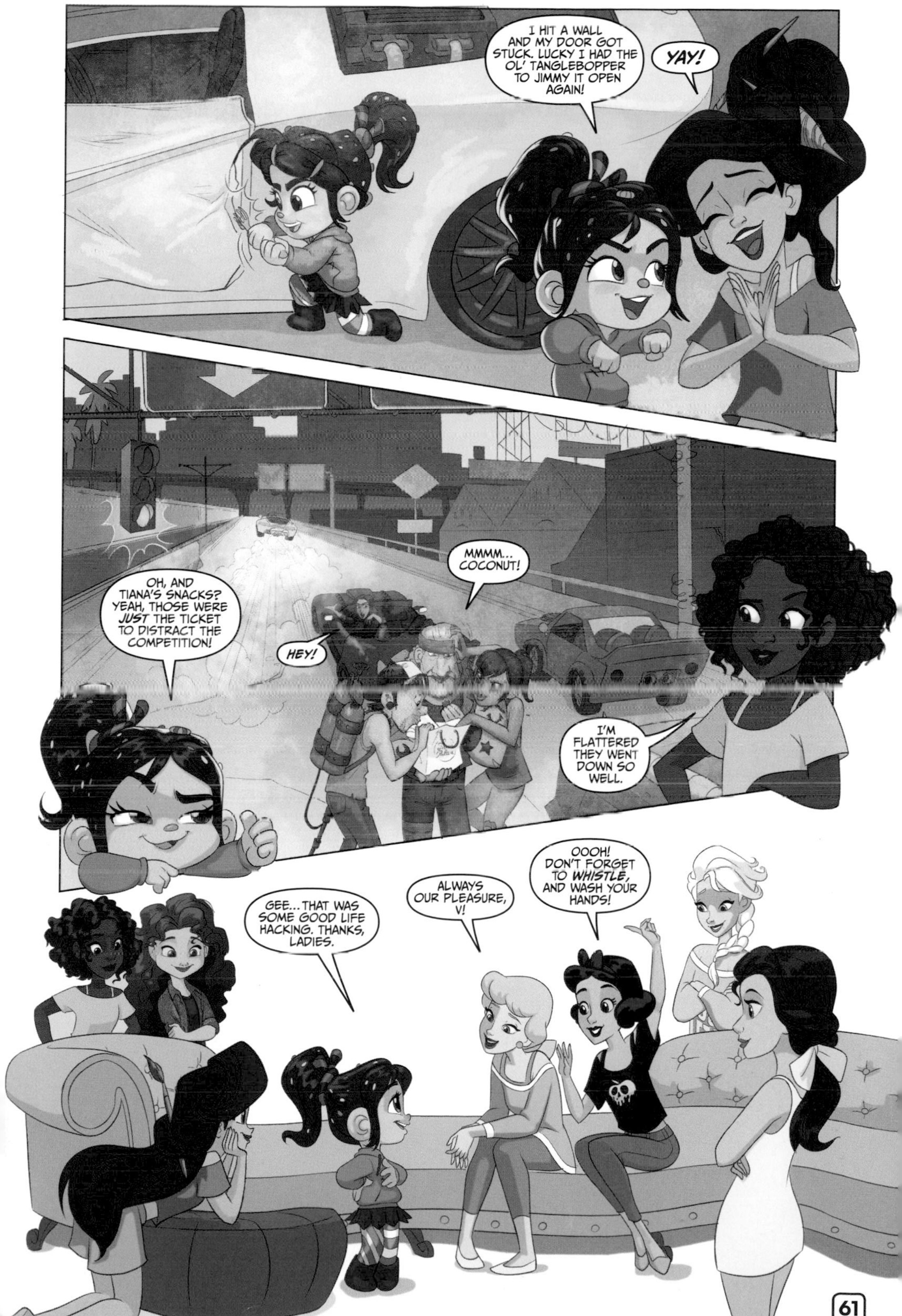

I HIT A WALL AND MY DOOR GOT STUCK. LUCKY I HAD THE OL' TANGLEBOPPER TO JIMMY IT OPEN AGAIN!
YAY!
OH, AND TIANA'S SNACKS? YEAH, THOSE WERE JUST THE TICKET TO DISTRACT THE COMPETITION!
MMMM... COCONUT!
HEY!
I'M FLATTERED THEY WENT DOWN SO WELL.
GEE... THAT WAS SOME GOOD LIFE HACKING. THANKS, LADIES.
ALWAYS OUR PLEASURE, V!
OOOH! DON'T FORGET TO WHISTLE, AND WASH YOUR HANDS!

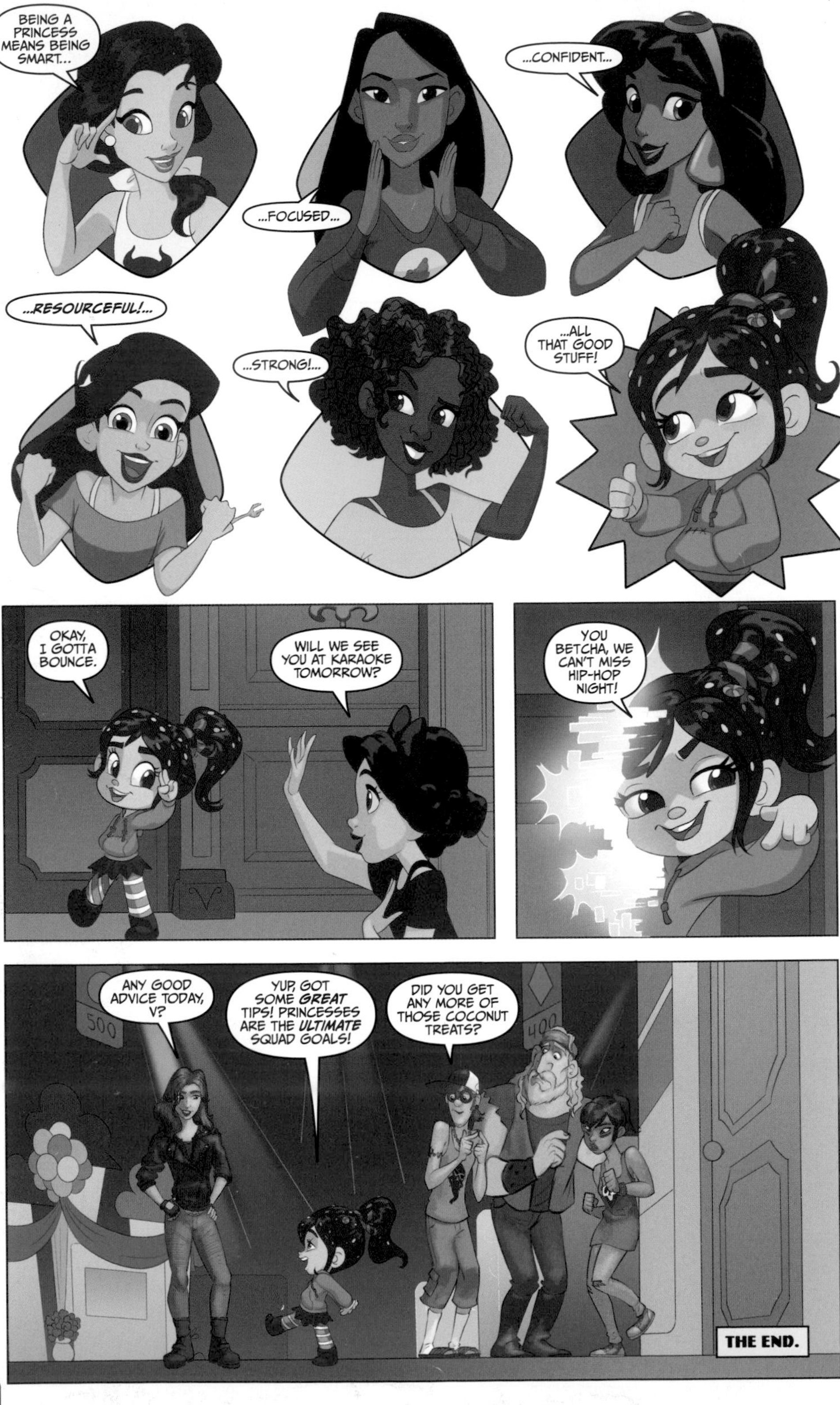

BEING A PRINCESS MEANS BEING SMART...
...FOCUSED...
...CONFIDENT...
...RESOURCEFUL!...
...STRONG!...
...ALL THAT GOOD STUFF!
OKAY, I GOTTA BOUNCE.
WILL WE SEE YOU AT KARAOKE TOMORROW?
YOU BETCHA, WE CAN'T MISS HIP-HOP NIGHT!
ANY GOOD ADVICE TODAY, V?
YUP, GOT SOME **GREAT** TIPS! PRINCESSES ARE THE ***ULTIMATE*** SQUAD GOALS!
DID YOU GET ANY MORE OF THOSE COCONUT TREATS?
THE END.

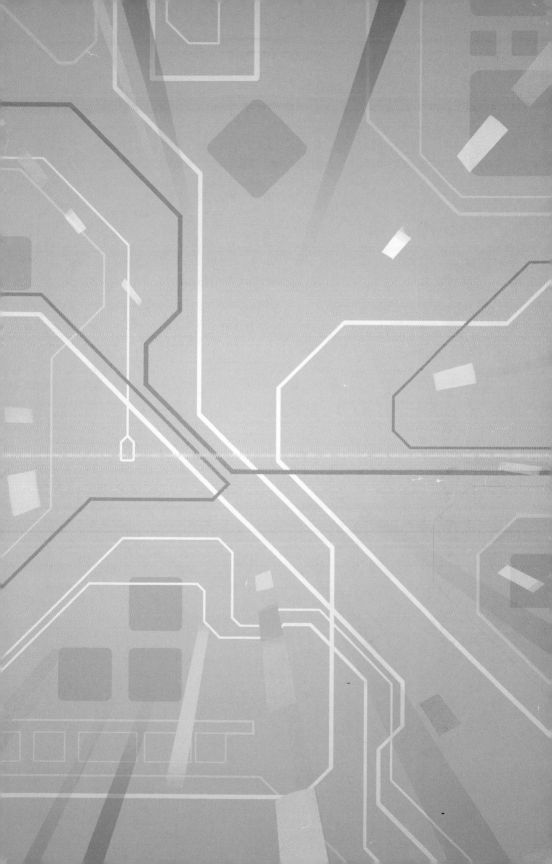

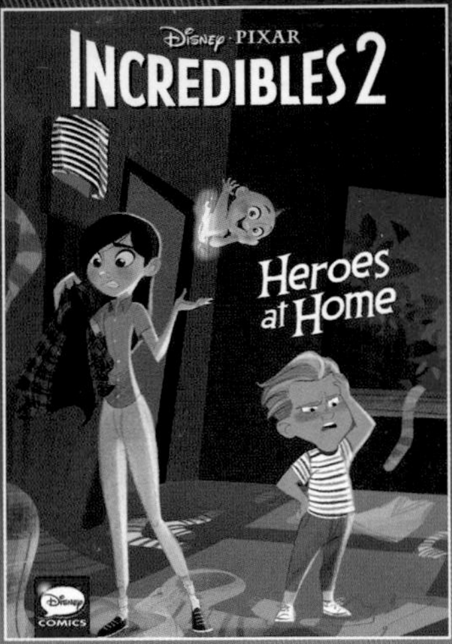
Disney · PIXAR
INCREDIBLES 2
Heroes at Home
Disney COMICS

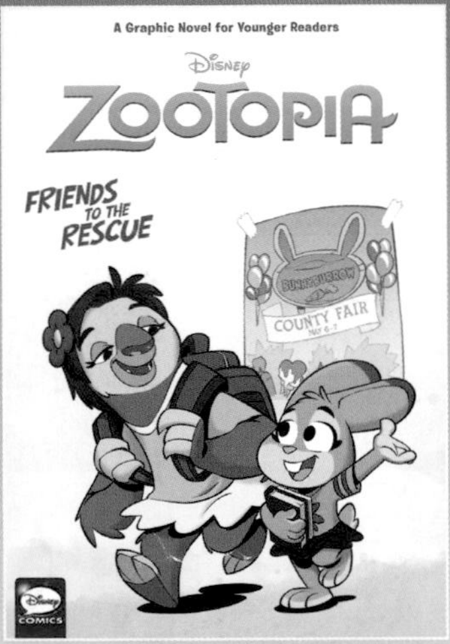
A Graphic Novel for Younger Readers
Disney
ZOOTOPIA
FRIENDS TO THE RESCUE
COUNTY FAIR
Disney COMICS

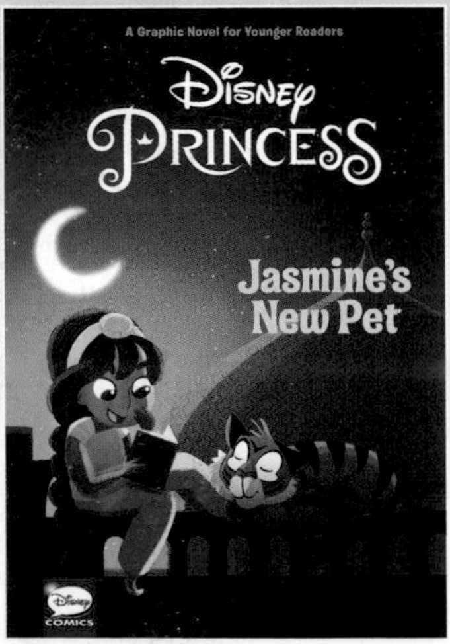
A Graphic Novel for Younger Readers
Disney
PRINCESS
Jasmine's New Pet
Disney COMICS

LOOKING FOR BOOKS FOR YOUNGER READERS?

$7.99 each!

EACH VOLUME INCLUDES A SECTION OF FUN ACTIVITIES!

DISNEY·PIXAR INCREDIBLES 2: HEROES AT HOME

Violet and Dash are part of a Super family, and they are trying to help out at home. Can they pick up groceries and secretly stop some bad guys? And then can they clean up the house while Jack-Jack is "sleeping"?

ISBN 978-1-50670-943-7 | $7.99

DISNEY ZOOTOPIA: FRIENDS TO THE RESCUE

Young Judy Hopps proves she's a brave little bunny when she helps a classmate. And can a quick-thinking young Nick Wilde liven up a birthday party? Friends save the day in these tales of Zootopia!

ISBN 978-1-50671-054-9 | $7.99

DISNEY PRINCESS: JASMINE'S NEW PET

Jasmine has a new pet tiger, Rajah, but he's not quite ready for palace life. Will she be able to train the young cub before the Sultan finds him another home?

ISBN 978-1-50671-052-5 | $7.99

AVAILABLE AT YOUR LOCAL COMICS SHOP OR BOOKSTORE! TO FIND A COMICS SHOP IN YOUR AREA, VISIT COMICSHOPLOCATOR.COM

DARK HORSE BOOKS

For more information or to order direct: On the web: DarkHorse.com | Email: mailorder@darkhorse.com
Phone: 1-800-862-0052 Mon.–Fri. 9 AM to 5 PM Pacific Time

Disney COMICS